The Yesterday Dilemma

Rocket Riders of the 27th Century

Book #3 of serial *Full Circle*

MICHAEL MOREAU

Copyright © 2019 Michael Moreau

All rights reserved.

ISBN-10: 1796226483
ISBN-13: 978-1796226485

DEDICATION

To those men and women who dared to think in new directions, inspire future next generations, and gift the world with visions of tomorrow. To all of the science fiction writers before me.

ACKNOWLEDGMENTS

My friends and family who have encouraged me to keep dreaming of impossible worlds.

1\\

As opposed to many of the worlds that the *Honshu* frequented Tersis was not a frontier planet or an uncharted, it was a prime world. Prime worlds were those that were considered to be thoroughly settled or were often the home-world of a space-faring civilization or, saving that, no less than a long-established colony. Despite humanity's unprecedented rapid expanse into the universe few human-founded worlds fell into the category, as the prime worlds that *were* colonies were often ones that had been established many centuries or even millennia, ago. That fact aside however there was hardly a prime world in known space without a significant human population. Mankind had done one thing better than any other species, and that was to adept to a variety of environments. It was the very reason that they were so numerous and now such a common sight on virtually every livable planet or outpost in known space.

It wasn't exactly *rare* for the ship to visit a prime world, mind you, but it also wasn't something they did weekly or even monthly either. Most of the *Honshu*'s work kept them ferrying cargo and escorting convoys between frontier worlds or making runs into uncharted territories.

Tersis was the fourth planet circling a yellow star very much like Earth's, from which it lied 96 light years distant. It had no native intelligent life but instead had been one of the colonies that had, two centuries previous, fought a protracted war for independence from Earth. Functioning as the primary base of operations for all rebel forces during the war it had grown into a densely populated planet in very short order. It was a charter member of the Federated Worlds and was a hub of trade and finance for many sectors of space. It was the type of place the crew might have looked forward to visiting for shore leave under different circumstances. This trip, on the other hand, was all about business, business of the none-too-pleasant nature. They were traveling to planet Tersis in search of the fugitive commander of Aeolus Station, Essa Von Braun.

"Police ships coming alongside sir." the pilot reported.

Outside of the cockpit windows the sleek shape of the police cruisers began to come into view. They were painted a clean cream color and had a system police logo emblazoned on the sides of their rounded bodies. These ships never entered atmo so they didn't have the large tall fins characteristic of most rocketships. They were designed purely for interplanetary flight, meaning no NC drive, and carried several shuttles to transport their crews to and from planetary surfaces. Tarsik smiled briefly. His first ship had been a retired old Novan police cruiser. It had rattled and squeaked and obviously kept him in-system but it'd been enough to get him into space.

"Wave coming in sir." Faust said, noticing the indicator on her controls light up.

"Put them through Pilot." the captain responded. He and Faust were still being quite short with one another.

The speakers in the cockpit crackled to life, fuzzy at first, as the ship's communications system attempted to fine tune the frequency. "Commander Arshan Rogers of Casidaen System Police cruiser 107. Please identify your vessel and registry number."

"R.S. *Honshu*, Novan registry 1017246." the captain responded.

The line remained silent for a moment while the cruiser checked their information. "Confirmed *Honshu*, proceeding with scan."

Several lights lit up on Herschel's now vacant console as the ship detected the police scan.

"Security scan clear. Welcome to the Casidae system *Honshu*."

Then, as suddenly as they'd come alongside, Tarsik and Faust could see the cruisers began to break off and within moments their running lights, flashing the ubiquitous red and blue of human police forces, were fading into the blackness of space.

"Now that that's done Faust I'll be in my quarters. Please make an announcement that Dr. Ramus' ceremony will go forward at 19:00 hours."

"Aye sir." was all that she replied.

The captain turned and left as soon as he'd received his acknowledgment. He still wasn't completely sure how to act around the pilot after recent events. He hadn't made up his mind yet as to whether he would discipline her or just let her stew in her own juices. Letting her live with the consequences of her own actions was likely better punishment than anything he could dream up. Should he choose not to take any punitive measures against her, however, it would be quite uncharacteristic of him. The captain usually followed up on what he said and did so with a very firm hand. His feelings toward Faust were also quite uncharacteristic though, she was the closest thing he'd ever had to an apprentice. Tarsik decided to wave the thoughts away, at least momentarily, as he entered the transport lift at the back of the cockpit and pressed the button for deck three. It lit up with a faint yellow glow in response to his touch.

They were still more than 6 hours out from Tersis and while the ship was perfectly capable of flying itself in a straight line on autopilot Emily Faust had never been one to leave her station. Shortly after the door on the transport whirred shut, however, she did just that. There was something she felt she had to attend to; a matter of conscience.

2\\

Three hours earlier…

"Holy shit!" the captain yelled as the immense hulk appeared directly in front of them.

They'd engaged NC in high orbit of Earth, 65 million B.C., so what was staring at them through the cockpit windows seemed impossible. It was the port side of the I.P.H.S. *Prometheus'* hull.

"Ansul *please* tell me my big gun is back online."

"Yes sir, you said to get everything fixed and we tried, but Captain we're in bad shape and firing that..."

"I'm not looking for approval Mr. Ansul. Stow it." with that Tarsik's hands danced over his console. He routed power away from non-essential ship's systems and targeted the *Prometheus'* portside engine-pod. "Firing in three, two, one..."

The *Honshu* in its entirety shuddered as the enormous Mark IX proton cannon fired. The giant red bolt it produced tore forth from the tip of the rocket's bow and in an instant ripped the *Prometheus'* engine from its mooring, breaking into glowing hot fragments of metal as it did so. Faust groaned as she pulled at the helm with all of her might, attempting to bank quickly enough to prevent a collision between the two craft. Once clear they all felt the jolt of force as Faust threw the engines into full-burn.

"Opening distance between us and *Prometheus* sir." she reported, "There's no way they're going to be able to give chase."

Tarsik took a moment to breathe before speaking. "Good. That means we don't have to worry about that damned vulcan cannon again." He looked over at Ansul who seemed to be every bit as surprised and shaken as he was from the whole affair. "Status Ansul?"

The Martian took a moment to examine the readouts coming from his display, the one that had until recently been the domain of Junior Pilot Herschel. "Looks like we blew a bunch of power relays exactly like I figured we would. Nothing I can't get fixed in a few hours though."

The look of relief on Tarsik's face was clearly visible to his first officer. He'd hesitated to fire the big gun knowing that they were already in bad shape. There'd been a small, but not insignificant, risk that they could have blown the entire ship's power systems, leaving them dead in space . In the end, however, he'd reckoned that the *Prometheus'* vulcan cannon was a much bigger danger to their lives than the potential for ship-wide power failure. They'd barely escaped getting their hull melted the last time they'd been in this place and engaging the NC drive inside of the Crux to escape the vulcan's plasma was what had thrown them back into the distant past in the first place.

Returning his mind to matters of the present he issued an order to his first officer. "Ansul get right on that. We don't know if we're going to be encountering any more IPH ships once we exit the Crux and I want the *Honshu* to be as ship-shape as she can be in case we end up in another tussle."

"You got it." Ansul stood and quickly rushed off to attend to his duties.

"Faust. Great flying as always. I'll be in my quarters making a call if you need me."

"Aye sir." she said to his back as he headed for the transport lift. She'd wanted to say, "Really? As always you big jerk?" but she maintained her composure.

When the door shut he was alone with his thoughts. How had they been sent back to the Crux? Then again, how had they ended up in the Cretaceous period in the first place? Maybe, he thought, when things settled down he'd contact a couple of scientist friends and relate to them the *Honshu*'s experience. Surely the phenomenon was worth proper study and someone could get a paper published off of the entire ordeal.

His mind floated back to the present. What about IPH? Were they going to pursue the *Honshu*? What were the true legal implications of all that had occurred on and in the vicinity of Aeolus Station?

A few moments later and the captain was at the door to his quarters. A quick thumb scan and the door opened with a whirr. Hanging his cape on a lamp he walked over to a display mounted on the wall and began to tap at the ivory-hued keys that lined the bottom edge of the device. He was looking through his list of contacts. One after the other their info-files and photographs slid onto the screen.

Tarsik was confident that he and his crew were on the right side of the law but better to confirm that fact. He was looking for Derian Leetus, his attorney. He had no idea what Leetus' local time was on Nova Terra so he decided a recorded message that could be delivered at a later time was best.

Just as his thoughts were gathered and he struck the key marked with the small red circle that would begin the recording there was a sudden interruption from his tele-wave. "Captain," it was Faust, "I've got a vid-wave coming in for you and you're not going to believe this…it's Deutron Cal."

The captain of the *Prometheus*? What could he *possibly*

want?

"Patch him through down here Pilot."

"Aye sir."

He quickly tapped the buttons to stop and erase his recorded message; one that would only show him talking to Faust over tele-wave and looking confused. A moment later the visage of Captain Cal appeared on the screen.

"Captain Tarsik."

"Yes. What do you want Captain, an apology for crippling your shiny new ship? If so then look elsewhere. You won't get one from me, not after firing that vulcan cannon at us."

Cal's head hung. "You must understand Captain, I detest that weapon as much as you do, but I was under direct orders to stop you using any and all means at my disposal."

"Orders from who? Essa Von Braun?" Tarsik asked cockily.

Cal raised his eyes and spoke, "Yes and Von Braun is precisely why I am contacting you *now*."

Tarsik raised an eyebrow, "Oh? Do continue." There was something in the way that Deutron Cal had uttered her name that told him IPH had finally gotten wise to her.

"She has fled the station in one of our executive shuttles. IPH has ordered me to pursue her but thanks to our little...run-in earlier today, the *Prometheus* is in no shape to intercept."

"So she ran?" Tarsik chuckled.

He nodded, "We confirmed your story about the illegal weapon and her being responsible for Lt. Okeke's death. When we tried to place her under arrest she fled."

"Wait..." Tarsik burst into laughter, "so you're wanting *me* to do your job for you and apprehend her?"

"Precisely Captain."

"You tried to kill everyone on my ship, not something I take kindly to Mr. Cal!" with that the Serviceman reached for the button to shut off the display.

"Wait! Captain I can understand your feelings. In fact I am the one who suggested *you* be the one contracted to capture her and I've been authorized by the IPH board of directors themselves to offer you an extremely generous compensation package."

"I'm listening." Tarsik tensed his lips in a visible sign of defiance but inwardly smiled at the notion of having IPH over the barrel.

"Due to the legal ambiguity of this entire...situation," Cal said plainly, "IPH wants to work with you to make it all right. You accept the contract to hunt down Essa Von Braun and bring her to justice and not only will you and your crew be handsomely paid but the board has also authorized a full refit of *Honshu* with the very latest tech at IPH's expense. They're also willing to wipe all records of what transpired on Aeolus Station." the man sighed, biting his lip, then stared Tarsik in the eye, "They're offering you a completely clean slate with IPH and neither of us have to get entangled in legalities. Sounds pretty good to me Captain. I'd take the offer if I were you."

Tarsik kept Cal waiting for some time before finally responding, "You will have my response within the hour." and with that he turned off the screen. He was going to take the contract, of course he was, he wasn't stupid. It was a chance to make some profit, get the ship fixed and updated, *and* take down Essa Von Braun all at the same time. His fellow captain had been correct, the deal was far too juicy to pass up. Still, it made him feel better to keep Deutron Cal and Interplanetary Holdings waiting for their answer.

3\\

Emily Faust sat on the deck of the torpedo bay. Her back was leaned up against the doctor's makeshift casket and her face buried into the palm of her own hands. She'd been crying for at least fifteen minutes and she didn't care if anyone found her there. Two men had died because of her decisions and there was absolutely nothing she could do about it; no way to atone for it. They were simply gone and she felt so completely powerless; more so than she ever remembered feeling at any other time in her life. Her conscience seethed with questions, ones that appeared to have no answers.

"I'm sorry!" she screamed as loud as she could in the small echo-filled metal room and then allowed herself to sob so heavily that it was all she could do to catch her own breath. "There's nothing I can do to bring you back. I'd give my life five times over if it would bring you back but I just can't. I've always been so careful, how could I have made such a huge mistake and cost you your life Doctor? I am so sorry and I just wish I could tell you that!"

She turned slowly to the casket and put her head down onto its lid. Strands of golden hair mixed with tears and stuck to her cheeks. "I don't *want* to have the life and death of others in my hands. I thought it was something that I could cope with, but I just can't. The captain was wrong about me, I'm *not* strong enough to lead others. When we get to Tersis I'm leaving the *Honshu* behind. I don't ever want to be responsible for another death. It's not something I can live with. At least if I'm out there on my own I won't get anyone else killed."

She laughed a little to herself. "Funny thing is...if you were here right now Doctor you'd have something smart to say. You'd try so hard to convince me that I *am* strong enough for this life." she let her voice drop to a whisper, "You'd be wrong though."

In an instant her face, still pressed up against the composite material of the torpedo casing, wrinkled into an expression of sheer confusion. She could see red light flashing, coming from the side of the casket and shining onto the material of her flight suit. A moment later the flashes were accompanied by a quick series of beeps, ones she was not familiar with. She'd never manned the torpedo bay and knew very little about the things.

Her eyes widened and she gasped as the sound of light tapping began to emanate from inside the casket. She jerked back as fast as she could and tried to get to her feet. Had her grief driven her insane? She ran to the transport and repeatedly tapped the button to open the door. Again there was tapping, this time louder.

"Not possible." she muttered under her breath. "That is *not* possible."

Tap. Tap. Tap.

She rubbed the tears from her eyes and ran over to the casket, her emotions in complete disarray. With trembling hands she unfastened the latch on its side and with a swift kick swung the lid open.

"Ah!"

The doctor's eyes were open and it appeared as though he was trying to speak. What's more, the wound on his neck appeared to be gone. What was happening? The pilot could only conclude that she must be asleep and having a nightmare. Were they still in that damned tree back on Earth, this whole thing a fevered hallucination?

"Faust." the weak man inside the casket cried out.

Emily screamed again and turned to run but caught herself. What if he really was alive and this wasn't a dream? What if the robo-doc had been wrong? She overcame her fear and knelt to his side.

"Doctor Ramus? By the great Galactic Serpent...you're alive!"

The man coughed loudly as he reached for the sides of the coffin and attempted to pull himself up. Faust quickly reacted and helped him into a sitting position. His eyes, though open, seemed glassy and he appeared to be extremely dazed and frail.

"Doctor how is this possible?"

"Laz..." he broke into a coughing fit and began to drool a bit. She tried to comfort him and when he finally caught his breath he looked up at her but decided not to speak. Instead he pointed to his head then brought the same hand down to his heart and made a pulsing motion with it like a beating heart.

"Doctor I don't understand."

"Laz..." he tried again through dry lips, "Lazarus node."

No sooner had he spoken the words then he went into another coughing fit. This time worse by far though and after a moment he seemed to go into convulsions.

Faust slapped her tele-wave, "Captain! Ansul! Somebody get down to the torpedo bay now! The doctor is *alive*!"

4\\

The captain shielded his good eye from the glare of Dathon VII's twin suns which hung high overhead and whose rays easily penetrated the thin yellow atmosphere that enveloped the high-gravity world. Small amounts of helium in the air, released from some underground mechanism that was beyond the captain's desire to understand, caused the Dathonian skimmers that flew overhead to emanate a very high-pitched sound that made him grit his teeth. Circling around the landing site the tiny craft appeared incredibly minuscule compared to the bulk of the captain's own rocket which stood like a gigantic green monolith protruding from the chalky desert floor.

"Exactly how are those tiny little things supposed to carry 24 tons of elorite half-way across this barren rock?"

The captain turned his head slightly toward the pilot who was coming down the loading bay ramp. He kept his good eye on the sky and presented her only with a partial grin and his eye patch.

"If the Sheikh had let us put down near his camp they wouldn't have to try and overload their century-old patrol craft. Just saying."

"You'll hear no argument from me Jones. I'd imagine

it's something to do with preventing his rivals from learning that he's accepting outside assistance with their little territorial dispute or whatever it is."

"What in space-blasted hell..." she had to pause momentarily to tie a cloth around her face. The skimmers were beginning to kick up a lot of dust and the arid soil of Dathon VII tasted of salt and sulfur. "Why in space-blasted hell would anyone be fighting over this dust-ball anyway?"

The captain chuckled, "Beats me Pilot. I never understood fighting over land, especially not when there's so much empty space out there."

"Yeah but not everyone has space in their blood like you and I do Captain. Some folks just can't live outside the suck." she replied, using the slang term that referred to a planetary gravity well.

"Yeah...well even then, there's tens of thousands of worlds a whole hell of a lot better than this one." he was beginning to have to raise his voice to speak over the high-pitched roar of antiquated engines, "I tried researching their little conflict before we landed but it looks like they're completely off the tele-net, so any records they keep aren't circulated. Best info I could find said their ancestors came here about two centuries ago on some kind of pilgrimage to find some sort of promised paradise."

The pilot sneered but of course the captain could not see the expression hidden beneath her makeshift scarf, "Let me guess, they pinned all of their hopes on deep-space probe readings and scraped together enough credit to purchase some outdated hulk they could convert into a colony ship, rode it all the way here, then found out that their probe data was nothing but a bunch of tark-snipe?"

The captain nodded. "Happened a lot back then Jones. Those probes could detect habitable worlds but they were pretty broad with their interpretation of exactly what that meant. FTL-capable probes were downright pricey a couple of centuries ago...if a potential group of colonists couldn't afford a follow-up mission they could, and often *did*, find themselves stranded on rocks like this."

"Yeah...," she countered, "so why fight *now*? Did you see any cities from orbit? Doesn't look like they're crowded for space if you ask me."

"Deliah." the doctor said as he made his way down the ramp behind them. He'd wrapped an expedition jacket around his head to keep the dust out, welding goggles covering his eyes.

"Care to explain?" the captain asked.

"There was a mission here by some historians about five decades back. Not much of their records survived after the Stellar Cartographical Society broke up a few years after the expedition but it would seem that finding themselves stranded on such a hostile world lead to the rapid evolution of the colonists' belief system. The explorers found that the first generation of Dathonians had demonized the outside universe, apparently so that their descendants would not have to suffer from the same burning desire to leave this awful place that they had. They created the legend of Deliah, a god-like woman who would someday descend from the heavens and turn their world into a lush and fertile one, the paradise promised them long before they set out for this planet. Like any strong belief system, however, differences quickly began to emerge in how it was put into practice."

"Leading to tribal conflict." the captain nodded his understanding.

"Precisely."

"Well," Pilot Jones interjected, "that could certainly explain why the sheikh would not wish to be seen dealing with us. They probably aren't supposed to have *any* contact with outsiders until their messiah arrives. I imagine the sheikh would have some explaining to do to the people of his tribe if they found out he were working with off-worlders willingly."

"A fair assessment I'd say." the doctor agreed, "What I

want to know is what use they could *possibly* have for such a large quantity of elorite."

Elorite was a rare and exotic mineral with unique properties, but not one that had any practical applications for either survival or warfare. Save for the skimmers and improvised weapons they used the Dathonians seemed to possess very little in the way of technology, certainly nothing that would require elorite in order to function or to be repaired. Hell, it hadn't even been discovered until several decades after the original colonists would have landed.

The grizzled captain could only shrug. A moment later the grating whir of the skimmer engines came to a halt and the dust began to settle down. The captain, the doctor, the pilot, and the auxiliary crewmen gathered at the base of the ramp watched as one after another the steersmen and their passengers jumped down from the ragged craft and landed on the hard ground, kicking up only a minimal amount of the near-toxic soil with their heavily worn boots. It was difficult to discern through their robes and the myriad of cloths they had tied around different parts of their bodies but it appeared as though two of the steersmen were female and three were male. One, the tallest male, wore an adornment of silver around his neck, and was the first to approach the rocket and the nega-grav sledges.

"Holrah fazil." the man spoke in a bizarre accent, "My name is Tamin, I am Third Mullah to Sheikh Mamad Al'taman."

The three officers bowed their heads slightly as a show of respect to the newcomer. At this the man smiled and looked around at the outworlders.

"Please. Lift your heads. Why is it that you bow in my presence?"

The captain bit his tongue. He did not wish to insult the Mullah but also wished to make it clear that his gesture was in no way meant to be submissive.

Tamin, however, cut him off before he could speak, "I

do not know your ways, but my goddess insists that no man or woman is greater than another."

The captain smiled and extended a hand. "What a refreshing notion. May I take it that it is not one shared by the other tribes on this planet?"

The tall native shook his head. His eyes, easily visible behind the orange-tinted acrylic of the visor he wore, squinted heavily. Then he spoke, "Unfortunately it is as you say. Many of the people of Dathon cling to ways that are long outdated. They are not wicked mind you, but they lack vision."

"Is *that* why you fight them?" the pilot blurted out. A quick look of horror from the captain told her that she'd stepped far out of line and would be receiving a tongue lashing once their guests had departed.

"I am sure that the concerns of this lonely world mean little to those who freely roam the stars." Tamin smiled. His face cracked with the wrinkles of a man thirty years his senior, the effects of a life lived with far too *much* sun and far too *little* moisture.

"It's a more fascinating place than you may imagine." the doctor spoke as he further descended the ramp towards the visitors.

"The situation on our planet is...complex." the stranger nodded. "Some are content to sit back and *wait* for the world to change. Others, like my people, wish to have an active role in helping it become a better place for our descendent."

"That's very noble." the pilot interjected.

"Thank you." Tamin smiled before turning back to the captain. "Now, may I assume that these sleds carry the mineral we negotiated for?"

"Indeed. If you don't mind me asking though, how do you plan on transporting it?"

Twenty minutes later the Servicemen stood in amazement, watching the Dathonian tribesmen lift off into the yellow sky with crates full of the rare mineral tethered underneath their skimmers by nothing more than handwoven nets of some fiber they did not recognize. It had taken them a remarkably short amount of time to secure their cargo and bid the off-worlders farewell. Tarsik offhandedly remarked to his crew members that they should take note of the native work ethic. They chuckled but Tarsik did not smile, he simply instructed them to get on with loading the sledges back into the ship.

The contract had been for delivery only, no pick up, so therefore had been brokered by an anonymous third party who would be responsible for payment now that it had been completed. Once everything was stowed they would break orbit and be on their way back to Nova Terra to collect the rather sizeable sum that had been negotiated.

As the whir of the skimmers faded into the distance, as if on cue, just when any and all possible risk of altercation had faded away, Carter Jones shuffled his drunken body down the ramp and put his arms around the pilot and kissed her on the back of the neck.

"Carter!" she exclaimed, "I'm working! Go back to our quarters and I'll be there in a little while."

"Yes ma'am!" he mocked a quick salute, to which she smiled and gave him a quick kiss before patting him on the rear as he walked back up the ramp with a grin.

The doctor had his face buried in his palm. He waited until Carter was well out of earshot before speaking. "I cannot for the life of me Emily fathom what it is you see in that...drunkard."

"What *I* can't fathom," the captain chimed in, "is how the best pilot I've ever seen...a young lady with immense potential...decides without warning to marry some buffoon she met loitering around a Novan casino."

The pilot blushed and wagged a finger at her crewmates, "I don't have to listen to this." I'm a grown woman."

"Actually...Emily, you *do* have to listen to this. After all, this is *my* ship and if you expect me to keep Mr. Good-

For-Nothing around you'd better make it clear to him that he's going to have to find some kind of way to pull his own weight."

"Or what?" she turned back to Captain Tarsik, who was rubbing sand out from under his eye patch. "You'll put us off-ship?"

There was a playfulness in her comment but still it raised the captain's ire. "Just get the damned ship ready to lift, we'll talk about this later Pilot."

With that she flashed a sarcastic grin and strode up the ramp. The feminine wiggle of her aft section did not escape the captain's attention. He could see why she would quickly come to the attention of someone like Carter Jones, what he *couldn't* understand was what attracted her to him. He was a wiry young fellow with an ugly scar on his cheek and constantly reeked of whatever cheap booze he had managed to lay hands on. Emily was smart and successful, if a bit brash and impulsive at times. Still, she didn't seem the type to take up with such a pathetic drifter, let alone marry him so quickly after meeting him.

"Then again," Tarsik thought to himself, "it's not like you have a history of healthy relationships yourself Harry."

"I don't understand it any more than you do." Doctor Ramus quipped, breaking the captain's reverie.

"She was drunk?" Tarsik posited, "Very...*very* drunk?" he laughed.

A dust storm was coming into sight far to the west and the sky was already beginning to darken. Taking notice of it Tarsik broke off his conversation with the doctor in order to yell at his men to get the sledges aboard and secure them for lift. He flapped his cape and turned for the ramp but just as he did so a familiar figure appeared at the top and called down to him.

"Captain, there's a strange communiqué that just came in over the tele-net. I think you'd better have a look." it was Junior Pilot Herschel, there was no mistaking the combination of dark skin and insecure tone of voice. Such a nervous young man.

"What do you mean?" Tarsik yelled back at him.

"I...well...you'll just have to see for yourself Captain. I don't know what to make of it."

Tarsik sighed and smiled at the doctor before jogging up the ramp. As per usual Herschel had little to say to his commander while riding the lift up to the cockpit. He was a good pilot and an extremely clever young man but he also had a severe lack of confidence, something that Tarsik found quite worrisome. Mrs. Jones had taken her seat in the pilot's chair by the time they arrived and had apparently taken note of the same odd wave that Herschel had discovered.

"Captain you're going to want to see this." she remarked.

"So I've been told." he glanced over at Herschel who was making his way over to the operations console to assume his station for lift-off then up at the pilot's screen. It appeared to be a contract. Tarsik walked over to stand next to the pilot's seat so that he could get a better look.

"What the hell?" he asked to himself, baffled.

"Exactly." both Herschel and Jones said in sync with one another.

"I never accepted that contract but there it is," he pointed, "my cipher is attached. That's impossible."

Every captain in the Service had a unique cipher that consisted of a 1.28 million character encrypted code that prevented anyone from faking his or her signature yet there it was, plain as day.

The captain's dark eye scanned the document quickly.

"Essa Von Braun?!" he exclaimed, then "Notes, bring up the notes Pilot."

With a couple of key presses the contract readout was replaced with a section containing the mission details. "What the space-blasted hell? We've never even *been* to Aeolus Station and I haven't seen Von Braun in years, didn't even know the bitch was out of prison!"

Tarsik turned and stormed away but before the transport doors closed Pilot Jones turned and asked, "Anything I can do Captain?"

"Just get us into space. I've got a call to make."

With that the doors slid closed.

5\\

"So what's the verdict Doc? Is it beyond all hope?" Tarsik asked.

Smiling up from his bed Yatin Ramus responded with a snide, "There's nothing wrong with your robo-doc Captain."

"Really?" Ansul chimed in, "Because it seemed awfully damned sure that you were dead Doctor."

The physician looked up at his friends, all of whom had gathered in the med bay to witness his miraculous resurrection with their own eyes. "It..." he began, "is something of a long story."

"Yeah, well we're sitting on a landing pad on Tersis, we've got a few minutes. Humor us." Tarsik ordered.

"You don't happen to remember a ship called the *Babylonia* do you?"

Tarsik wrinkled his brow in thought. A moment later Ansul poked his finger into the captain's arm and blurted out, "That bad business with the Mercadian junkers!"

"The old Earth ship they were trying to pick apart?" Tarsik replied. The affair with the *Babylonia* was not something that one could too easily forget. "That would be the one." Ramus groaned heavily as he attempted to sit up. "If you'll recall Captain you and your crew very bravely refused to allow the junkers to salvage her."

"There was nothing brave about it. Those were active stasis pods on-board and Mercadians don't have a whole lot of regard for life when there's salvage involved. They would have shot those pods into space and never given it a second thought."

"Well..." Ramus continued, "it took some time to come to terms with the reality of things but let's just say that my coming aboard as the *Honshu*'s doctor was not completely by chance."

The notion Tarsik was beginning to foster made little sense so he decided to simply get to the heart of the matter. "I don't like mystery stories Doctor, spit it out."

The captain then remembered his manners, as well as the present condition of the man he was speaking to. "Please."

Yatin shook his head gently in agreement and cleared his throat before proceeding. "You see, there were, if you recall, seven of us in stasis." he watched as Tarsik bit his lip in thought and Ansul's eyes went wide. Faust's did as well, though she was at the back of the room and a bit harder for the doctor to see clearly with the bay's lights muted such as they were. "The *Babylonia* was the only ship to escape our base on Septus Minor when the colonials attacked. Out of nowhere..." the doctor seemed to stare out into space, "a fleet so large it blanketed the sky and us with little more than a few defense batteries and a couple of transports."

"This is...unreal." was all that Ansul could mutter. He turned away and shook his head, "That's just not possible Doc."

Tarsik was thinking the same thing, they had onboard their ship a living specimen from the Colonial Wars, one that had been their friend for the last few years no less!

"We tried to provide cover for the *Ganges*, she was the

larger of the two ships and was carrying our civilian staff, but a lucky missile took out her engines and we watched in horror as she fell from the sky. Over three hundred people were aboard that ship."

Faust looked away and covered her mouth, trying to mask the look of shock that had come over her.

"We didn't make it out unscathed either, however, and after narrowly escaping the outpost we found ourselves adrift." he was still staring off blankly, his voice nearly trembling. "The uh…the hibernation pods were our only option." he looked up and tried to fake a smile for his friends. "There…there weren't enough of them though. Five men stayed awake, watching over the rest of us until…well until they had no oxygen left.

No one said anything. The room was deathly quiet. Space was a rough place and death not something far from the minds of most spacers but the crew gathered to hear the doctor's story could not imagine the types of sacrifices that war-time called for. Tarsik imagined those men trapped aboard a floating hulk, slowly running out of breathable air, and not daring to signal other humans for help for fear that they would be enemies who would capture or kill their compatriots.

"None of us" the doctor continued, "could have imagined that many decades later our ship would be stumbled upon and nearly ripped apart by Mercadians for scrap. It was very luckily for us that a Service crew, that of the *Honshu*, came along and prevented such a tragedy." he looked up at Tarsik, "You see after I spent some time coming to terms with the new world in which I found myself I sought you out Captain."

Ramus reached out and grasped Tarsik's hand and gave it a healthy squeeze.

"You and your people had saved my life and those of my fellow soldiers, I felt it only right to try and repay my debt the only way I could, with my services as a physician."

"And a cut of the haul?" Ansul jested, to which the

doctor only smiled. Lying there on the bed in med-bay there was still little color in him and there were a multitude of monitors and tubes attached to him, all fitted by the robo-doc of course.

"So what's the deal Doc?" Tarsik quipped, "You basically immortal thanks to that...what'd you call it in your head?"

"Lazarus Node." Faust spoke up from her position at the far end of the room.

"Yes, Lazarus Node." Doctor Ramus nodded in her direction, "And no, I'm afraid it's a one-shot deal Captain." he said to Tarsik plainly. "Every soldier in the Legionary Forces had one implanted into their skulls. Miraculous devices but I'm afraid they take quite a toll on the body though. It may have brought me back from the dead but thanks to all of the adrenaline it released I won't be sleeping for several days, no matter how many sedatives the robo-doc prescribes. It's also probably taken half a decade or more off of my lifespan...but that seems a small price to pay I suppose, given the alternative."

"Seeing as how you're not dead anymore, yeah, I'd say so." Ansul smiled and stepped closer to the doctor's bed. "Guess we're going to have to keep all of this quiet unless we want to be fighting off waves of frantic historians trying to nab your ass for the Smithsonian Planet's collection eh?"

Faust remained against the wall. A combination of shame and disbelief made it very difficult for her to deal with the situation. Even as the door to med-bay whirred open and crewmen Fizril and Jones walked in, both with smiles plastered across their faces, the pilot could not bring herself to follow suit, which was really saying something since the *smile* that Fizril wore looked comically like that of a house cat bearing its fangs. During the ensuing conversation she managed, albeit briefly, to lock eyes with the doctor. The Martian noticed and barely managed to stifle a chuckle but Emily paid it no attention.

She hoped that her look conveyed the true sorrow she felt for having nearly, no for having *actually*, gotten Ramus killed. She turned her head from those huddled around the doctor's bedside and shortly thereafter left without saying a word. Had she bothered to look back she would have caught sight of the older man's glance, it was a look of forgiveness aimed directly at her but one that missed its mark by only a fraction of a second.

Ignoring those who addressed her in the hallways she proceeded straight to her cabin whereupon she packed a bag with the few things she felt she truly needed before recording a quick message to the captain. Pressing her Federated Worlds issued ident-badge into the terminal next to the screen she then transferred all of her accrued pay from the *Honshu*'s safe-deposit, tucked the badge into her bag, and walked out of the room. A quick glance back, before the doors closed themselves behind her, nearly brought a tear to her eye but she would not allow it.

6\\

As they stepped down onto the reflective polished metal of the landing pad Tarsik turned to address his first officer. The Martian had a particularly sarcastic smirk on his face and was wearing his Service uniform as opposed to his more typical mechanic's outfit. He was also wearing his cape, crookedly, but still. The captain attempted his most macho of forms as he leaned in to fix it.

"Oh c'mon Harry. You really gonna groom me like my mother right here in front of..." he turned, expecting some of the auxies to be following them, "Wait, are they not coming?"

"Nope. I was lucky enough to arrange a meeting with an adjunct security minister...Mr. Felize or something like that, and I think it a little more professional to visit his office without any of our more..." he searched for the word, "*rough around the edges*...colleagues in tow."

At that Ansul laughed. "Oh yes, you and I being the *pinnacle* of sophistication and refinement and all."

Tarsik chuckled mildly.

"Okay Harry, I think you've got it. Stop hovering." he said as he swatted the captain's hand away from his collar to which Tarsik only glared disapprovingly.

"These here are civilized folks Mr. Ansul, not some back-water savages.

"May I assume from the fact that your hair is nicely tamed and that you've pulled something out of your closet other than your tattered old yellow cape that this adjunct minister is of the female variety?"

"Hah! You can assume that if you like but you'd be wrong." Tarsik sneered.

Ansul raised an eyebrow.

"Okay...the assistant who arranged the meeting was, however, female and quite a looker." the captain replied.

"Then...why are you so intent on making *me* look good? What if she has a thing for Martians?" Ansul smirked.

With no one around to witness a moment of playfulness Tarsik patted his friend on the shoulder before giving him a mild, but noticeable, little jab in the ribs. Ansul followed up with a punch to the chest and immediately went into a shifty-foot fighting stance.

"We really gonna fight over a girl we've never even met? You remember what happened last time we competed for the affections of a lady, right?"

Tarsik laughed and swatted at Ansul, catching him on the upper part of his right arm. "Yeah, we both got rejected, then ended up getting so wasted on Kitarian Whiskey that we woke up in the back of a garbage transport."

"Hey what's that?" Ansul pointed at something behind the captain.

Tarsik turned to look but didn't fall for the ruse. He jumped as the Martian tried to sweep his legs then countered with a quick and playful knock to the top of the head.

"Hey, careful there!" Ansul scowled, "You almost knocked my goggles off. You *really* wanna be guiding me around this place like a service-dog for the next couple of hours?"

"So..." came a voice from the top of the ramp, "you

two got somewhere to go or did you just get all dressed up to come out here and play grab-ass?"

The two officers jumped to attention so fast they nearly pulled muscles. Tarsik immediately went back to straightening Ansul's cape.

"That's sweet, really." Jones beamed sarcastically.

Through gritted teeth the captain responded, "Crewman Jones you keep on sticking your nose where it doesn't belong and I'll have to put you off the ship." he then looked straight up at him and grinned, "Or promote your ass so I don't have to worry about being myself in front of an auxie."

Jones belted out a hearty laugh.

"You'd have to slap the bottle out of his hands first Cap." Ansul quipped.

The crewman waved them away and turned to walk back up into the loading bay.

"You know we joke but I do feel that lately I've compromised myself more than I should in front of the lower crewmen."

"You're a person Harry, it's okay to act like one."

"Wrong, I'm a Service Captain first and foremost. When we get back to the ship I'm going to have to shake things up a bit and show them I'm still every-bit the massive hard-ass I've always fashioned myself as."

"It's really just Jones and Fizril that've seen the more relaxed side of you lately Harry and neither of them seem the type to go blabbing all over the ship that you're not as big of a toughie as you look. I would venture to say that most of the men are still terrified of you...in fact maybe being a little more relaxed could be a good thing?"

Tarsik looked off at the city skyline, "No Ansul, that's you. They see *you* as a friend, always ready with a joke or a smile but ready to kick them in and backside if they slack off on their duties. Me they see as the implacable commander and that's just how it needs to stay."

Ansul reluctantly nodded in agreement. "I guess so."

The two looked over at the transit tube, waiting to catch sight of the transport that was supposedly on its way to pick them up. Looking around it dawned on them that Tersis was probably about the cleanest place that the *Honshu* had visited in some years. Even compared to many other prime worlds it was pristine. The capital city, which once carried the name of Resolute during the colonial wars and for some time after, was now known as Serenity City. It was an awe-inspiring place, a beautiful mix of high technology and nature. Every nook, crevice, and alcove featured some type of potted plant or lovely sculpted tree. Many of them were imports from Earth but some were of the local variety as well. The difference between the two was easy to distinguish. The indigenous flora of Tersis featured leaves of blue and peach colored hues and often grew into more delicate, spindly branches than most of the off-world varieties.

All of the buildings were of a soft white or light grey color and most towered into the sky. It was a sky that featured the magnificent sight of the giant ringed planet, Lorandis, looming large over the horizon. Despite the two planets having an unusually close orbital path, less than 100 million kilometers, Tersis remained habitable for two main reasons. Firstly it had no large oceans to be pulled around by the gravitational force, causing horrendous tsunami. Tersis' water, about 35% of the surface, was instead locked up in a series of lakes scattered about the surface. Secondly Lorandis, despite being some 20% larger than Jupiter, was an extremely low-mass planet, exerting only about two Earth gravities.

Travel about the city was provided for primarily by a series of transport tubes which magnetically levitated small spherical pods through vacuum chambers at high speed. Tarsik and Ansul had seen similar systems on several other worlds but apparently the one on Tersis was newer and more refined than those, for it took less than a minute once they boarded the pod to cover what must have been several kilometers of twists and turns. As the pod, comfortably appointed with a soft beige interior, rocketed through the city they watched in amazement as it would pass right through buildings and at one point even dipped underground to pass under the river that bifurcated the city. Upon coming to a stop the little machine produced a soothingly mellow "boong" sound and the doors slid upon without a sound.

In stark contrast to the somewhat hodge-podge and nearly zany appearance of the city's buildings from the outside, beside their uniform color, the place in which the two rocket-men found themselves had a sleek and austere look. A governmental office, there was no doubt about it. Through the round doorway of the lift they were greeted with the sight of a grand hallway some 20 or so meters in length. The floor was of a brown marble and the walls, slanted up to a high ceiling, looked to be made of something akin to granite. The two stepped from the lift and noticed how the mag-plates on their Service boots rang out on the cold stone floor. The sound echoed through the passage and they saw a head rise to peer at them from behind the counter that stood at the opposite end of the hall. There was a large wooden desk of the finest quality that stood framed between two large stone columns that slanted back at about a 15 degree angle until they reached the ceiling.

Both men pressed buttons on their belts that retracted the mag-plates in their boots, so as not to scuff the fancy floor that had no-doubt cost the taxpayers of Tersis quite a pretty penny. They passed a couple of law officers headed for the lift as they approached the desk, all of which tipped their hats gently. Tarsik and Ansul nodded in response and greeted them with respect. As they drew nearer to the receptionist they could see that she was an older Koti female, her brown head speckled with yellow spots and her pig-like nose wrinkling as her eyebrows furrowed. That nose held up a pair of spectacles, a peculiar sight in the modern age.

"May I help you?" the Koti woman asked in a scratchy voice as they walked up and rested their hands on the counter.

"Yes. We have a meeting with Adjunct Minister Felize." Tarsik stated matter-of-factly. He was quite disappointed that the attractive young lady he'd booked the appointment with was nowhere to be seen.

"Hmm." the woman grunted and then looked down at the computer terminal in front of her. Her six-fingered hands went to work busily tapping at its keys. After a few moments she apparently became aware of the mens' impatience. "Mint?" she asked as she lifted a small glass bowl from her desk onto the counter-top.

Ansul managed a better smile than his captain did and was the only one to accept the offer. Quickly the receptionist went back to hacking at the keyboard and after what seemed like another absurdly long stretch of time she looked up at the two Servicemen through her spectacles.

"You're early." she grunted.

Tarsik pulled his timepiece from his belt and looked at it. "Actually we're two minutes late. Our appointment was for 13:00 hours."

"Hmmph." the Koti grumbled, "First time on Tersis?"

"Yes...why?"

"It's custom here to always schedule appointments fifteen minutes early."

"Why?" Ansul asked, looked quite puzzled.

"So that you're not late!"

"But if everyone knows that wouldn't they just arrive fifteen minutes later?"

"Hmmph." she grumbled again, "Take a seat and the Minister will be with you shortly.

To their left was a set of four chairs placed neatly by a large window that overlooked the city. They were high quality and appeared to be crafted with some sort of leather, with arms made of some expensive and exotic hardwood. Ansul and the captain did as they were told and plopped into two of the seats. They were magnificently comfortable and the two exchanged looks of pleasure.

"Well, I've got no idea whether or not this guy has anything that'll be helpful in finding Von Braun but he sure as hell knows how to pick furniture."

"Speaking of Von Braun," Ansul started, "when we *do* catch up to her, is it going to be a shoot-on-sight kind of situation?"

The captain stirred in his chair, "I know you'd prefer not to have to kill anyone old friend, and despite our history with her I'd prefer not to have to kill her either, but you know as well as I do that she won't give us much of a choice. If it comes down to putting my men in harm's way trying to take her in or simply taking the easy way out and vaporizing her on the spot I'm going to choose the second option."

Ansul nodded his understanding. "You know if I have to I *will* kill her."

"I know that Ansul."

"The minister will see you now." called the scratchy voice of the little old Koti secretary. They hadn't been seated more than thirty seconds and couldn't help but feel that somehow the woman was having some fun at their expense. "Straight down the hall."

Ansul made a concerted effort to eyeball the woman as they walked past, she let out a little huff and turned back to her work. The hallway continued behind the large reception desk for about another 10 meters and ended with a set of tall glass doors which slid open silently as Tarsik and his first officer stepped from the marble floor onto the carpet of the minster's circular office. Despite only being an adjunct minister his space was at least 10 or 12 meters in diameter and was furnished as nicely as the rest of the building that they'd seen thus far. Everything was of a soft grayish-blue color and was immaculately clean. The minister, or at least who they presumed to be the minister, turned from the large window behind his desk overlooking the city to greet them as they stepped forward.

"You must be Captain Tarsik." the man said as he exchanged a firm handshake from across his desk.

"I am, and this is my XO, Ansul." he said, introducing the Martian, who's hand the minister shook next.

"Please, have a seat and make yourselves comfortable gentlemen. Can I get you anything? We have some lovely Mekta-Spice tea that just came in from Corinor."

Both of the spacers chuckled to themselves.

"No, thank you." Tarsik replied.

"Have I said something wrong?" the man asked.

"Absolutely not." Tarsik said, returning to his steely yet respectful demeanor. "We meant no insult Minister...you *are* Minister Felize correct?"

"Oh. Yes. How impolite of me. My name is Hernando Felize and I am Adjunct Security Minister for Tersis and the entire Casidae system."

"Nice to meet you Minister. We were laughing about the Mekta tea because *we* were the ones that negotiated trade rights with the Corinite about three years ago."

"Oh, well that's excellent. I can tell you their teas are quite the sensation here on Tersis. I'm afraid I don't know much about their world though, are they a friendly people?"

The captain said nothing, trying to hold back a grin, finally Ansul spoke. "Strong alcohol...powerful women."

With that the minister allowed a smile to light up his face as he chuckled to himself. "Very different than here then I'm afraid. Most of the states here on Tersis are prohibition states and our women are quiet and polite."

"Not that one out there." Ansul joked as he pointed toward the hallway.

"Did Tragelda give you a hard time? The Koti have a very strange sense of humor. I've talked to her several times about it."

"Minister I have to put up with a Martian all day, every day, I think I can handle a sour old Koti." Tarsik stated.

Felize looked over at Ansul, as if to gage whether or not he'd been insulted by his captain's remark. He had not been. After a moment he seemed to snap back into bureaucrat mode.

"So, as to the business which brings you here. I've been contacted by a representative of Interplanetary Holdings and have been told that you are pursuing a fugitive by the name of Essa Von Braun."

"Can I assume that IPH also arranged to have some of your engineering corps take a look at my ship and perform some quick repairs, on their tab of course?"

"Yes." he nodded, "They've also informed me that after you've completed your assignment that you'll be putting in to the Lorandis orbital docks for a full refit, again at their expense. They must consider you quite a valued associate to be going the extra kilometer like that."

Good, IPH hadn't mentioned anything of the sketchy business on the station.

"Oh yes, they adore us." Ansul let slip with only the slightest hint of visible sarcasm.

"You'll forgive my bluntness," Tarsik cut in, hoping to prevent Felize from analyzing Ansul's response, "but I have to assume that since we're meeting in person you've got some relevant data on Essa Von Braun's whereabouts."

"Absolutely," the minister beamed, "let me pull up what we've got." he tapped at some keys on his desk and a little spherical robo dropped from a hidden alcove in the ceiling and came to hover near his left shoulder. A moment later it made a soft humming sound and then a holographic screen appeared a short distance in front of it.

"Thank you El-7." Felize said, apparently addressing the little robo, for it immediately detached the small sphere from its center that was projecting the hologram and flew back up into the alcove. "He's my personal assistant" the minister smiled, "Don't know what I'd do without him. Have you seen an El-series before?"

Both men shook their heads and Tarsik responded, "I'm afraid most of the places we visit don't have access to the latest tech. Your little robo reminds me of something though. We recently lost our scouters on a mission. Is there any chance your quartermaster could supply us with a couple of replacements?"

"I don't see why not," the minister shrugged, "what were they, Mark VIs?"

"Mark IIIs." Ansul replied.

"Well, we'll see if we can load you out with a few of the Mark VIs as part of your refit eh?"

"Thank you Minister."

"It's my pleasure. Now, to answer your question about the data we've got on Von Braun." he turned to the screen, with a couple of key-taps it brought up a rotating slideshow of information. "Shortly before you landed we picked up the IFF code, albeit only very briefly, of the ship that IPH claims Von Braun stole from their facility. It was on the scanner-net that we have installed out at the edge of our system. If I had to guess I'd say that she didn't expect it to be as sensitive as it is and as soon as she realized she was being tracked she disabled it."

"Makes sense," Tarsik started, "Casidae is the nearest system from..." he almost mentioned Aeolus but then caught himself, "...her last known position. From what I understand she's in a small craft with a very limited NC-horizon so it'd make sense for her to try and ditch it for something a little faster as soon as she could."

"My thinking precisely Captain."

"The question is, where would she go? Seeing the security in orbit there's no way she could land an unregistered craft here on Tersis. Anywhere else in the system she might be able to put down?"

The minister shook his head. "To be honest there's a

very short list of locations in the Casidae system where she *might* be able to set down without being queried by our police patrols." he tapped some keys and the display changed yet again, this time is showed what looked like an inhabitable moon. "This is Casidae VIIF. It's a satellite of our outermost planet. Breathable air, some basic plant life, no colonies however due to high levels of radiation emanating from the host planet. There's an abandoned base there that used to be manned by the system police but piracy on our borders has dropped off significantly in the last couple of decades so we retired it about five years ago. Von Braun's heading, at the time we first detected her, was in the general direction of Casidae VII."

"Let me guess, she changed course before turning off her IFF?"

"You got it." Felize confirmed, "A simple trick that I think we both agree fools no one."

Tarsik nodded. "Still, you said there are other places."

"Perhaps, but VIIF would by far be the easiest for her to access. With the other locations she'd run about a 50/50 chance of being held for questioning, especially since we put out an APB on her."

"If that's the case," Ansul jumped in, "then I think we can assume she's going to meet with someone."

The minister looked confused. "Possibly, but how can you be so certain?"

The Martian leaned in closer before continuing, "If she was detected heading for the moon and attempted such a simplistic ruse as changing her course before disabling the IFF then it means that she *has* to go there. Now don't get me wrong, no one will accuse this woman of being a genius, but she's far smarter than that. No, she knew we wouldn't be fooled by her veering off course tactic but knows it likely won't matter since she'll have made her rendezvous and have gotten away before we make it there anyway. At best her little ruse was a shot in the dark to throw anyone pursuing her off her scent just long enough to make that meeting. Besides, if not a rendezvous then what would her plan be, to just sit there until she's forgotten about?"

Both the minister and Captain Tarsik nodded in agreement.

"That presents us with something of a problem." Tarsik commented. "If she's got a pre-arranged meeting then she won't be there for long. The *Honshu* doesn't need that much in the way of repairs but with the beating she's taken I'd have to imagine it will be at least a day before we can be underway. Essa may be gone by then and her tracks will be cold."

"I concur. In fact I dispatched a police cruiser to the base as soon as I received this information but they were pulled away on an errand of mercy to help a passenger ship that is in distress. I was about to arrange for another ship to head out that way. You two gentlemen would, of course, be welcome to join them."

Tarsik and Ansul exchanged glances. Then the captain spoke, "You do that Minister. When can we leave?"

"I should think within a couple of hours if that suits you."

"It does." Tarsik said as he rose from his chair quickly followed by his second in command. He reached out and shook the minister's hand. "I thank you for all of your assistance Minister. Please excuse us while we go and make preparations."

"Yes. It was very nice to have met the two of you. I will have an orbital shuttle meet you on the *Honshu*'s docking platform as soon as one is available."

With that the Servicemen turned for the door, capes flapping as they did so.

"Please let me know if there is anything else you require Captain." Minister Felize spoke to their backs.

"Just make sure my ship is ready! If Von Braun flees the system I want to be able to go after her." Tarsik said without turning around.

7\\

Faust always swore she'd never again deal with a Prilt but she found herself in the disorganized warehouse of a particularly ugly and odorous one called Stors. As far as she was concerned the Prilt were an entire species of thieves and con artists. Emily liked to think herself someone who didn't judge superficially but in many years of dealing she couldn't recall ever meeting an honest one. They just seemed to have a knack for hoarding junk and eventually finding an off-world sucker to pass it off on for a profit.

As she watched the squat little furry creature, clad in what she could only describe as oily rags, push his way through the mess she wondered if it was the result of some kind of social evolution. Did the Prilt just find their niche in galactic society and fill it so well that it became what was expected of them? What was their home-world like? If they all kept as much junk as the ones she'd met then it must be a very cluttered place.

"It's just pass this stack of condensers." Stors belted out. Prilt physiology seemed to make it incapable for them to speak in any manner other than a harsh yell. Even then their Standard had a strange accent that was difficult to understand. His flat little face and large eyes that seemed as though they would fall from his head turned to the human. "You going to help or should I do all the work myself?"

"Move." was all she said to him. She'd learned that the best way to deal with his kind was to be very straightforward. Unlike Mercadians, who loved to salvage anything they could and then try to swindle their customers, the Prilt tended toward harsh honesty. They didn't seem to have a good understanding of subtlety or sarcasm and also never seemed to be terribly skilled at deception.

For years she'd blamed one of their kind for substandard parts that had caused her to lose her father's tug on one of the moons of Casalgrand but she had come to understand that incident had been her fault.

She'd told the Prilt she'd bought the parts from, Lon, that she'd wanted the "cheapest working parts" he had. Being quite literal that's exactly what she'd gotten. The little junk dealer had gone through the cheapest parts he had and found ones that still worked. He never specified that they likely needed immediate reconditioning because in his strange little alien mind they still "worked" like she had specified. The Prilt simply were not chatty, nor did they volunteer information. They gave you exactly what you asked for, no more, no less. It was annoying but once you understood that fact you might be able to get a decent deal from one.

Faust grunted as she tossed aside the long cylindrical condensers that looked as though they'd come from something at least a century old, possibly more. Stors snorted angrily as one of them nearly hit him in the head as she tossed them aside. She flashed him a quick smile that said "See, stay out of the way".

Once she'd managed to move enough of them the two were able to make their way between a half-torn-apart sky taxi and the ancient Type-3 rocket hull plate that was blocking their path. Stors' warehouse was immense, something on the order of 300 meters wide by at least that much again long.

Their path cleared and the little Prilt pushed past Emily and strode out into the "clearing". He grinned as he pointed to a small craft, mostly intact, that looked as though it had been accumulating dust for some time. It was long and narrow, blue in color with a silver belly that looked very much out of place. Its port-side landing strut seemed to be missing some parts so it laid at an angle but Faust could see that the cockpit and most of the fuselage looked to be in good condition.

"What?" she scoffed, "This is what you made me trudge through a veritable jungle of trash to see?"

"Hmmph." the little Prilt wrinkled his flat nose then shuffled on short legs around to the back of the craft. "Casidaen Starworks F-Type intra-solar rocket transport. One of the fastest atmosphere-capable ships ever made, in your budget at least." he grinned and pointed up, "See, big engines."

"Stors I should punt you into one of these mountains of trash!" she said, pointing around at all of the debris that littered the floor of the warehouse, "I said I wanted an interstellar ship, not a damned rock-hopper."

The little junk dealer said nothing, he merely smiled and waved her on as he began to wade back into the scrap pile.

"No no no, come back here Stors! Look, I'm sorry about what I said to you, but I was serious about what I want."

He turned back and looked at her with those huge black eyes, "Just come with me girl. You see."

Emily let out an exasperated sigh but decided to humor him. This time they didn't go far before reaching another spot where the junk thinned out and Stors turned to her with what she could only assume was a satisfied grin on his flat little face as he pointed to yet another heap of junk lying on the deck.

"And this is?" she asked.

"Another reason F-Type is best. Interstellar module for ship."

"What?"

"Hmmph." he grunted once again, then shuffled over to Faust, "Module stays in orbit, ships flies to surface. When ship returns it docks with module. Module has NC!"

Though it was a fairly rare configuration Faust had seen it before on alien vessels but never on one that was human-manufactured. She liked to think of it as some kind of wacky "dealer option" that basically allowed the manufacturer to sell you two ships instead of one. A novelty more than anything else.

"So, what you think?"

"I don't know Stors. You'll have to give it to me for a hell of a good price seeing as how I'm going to have a lot of repairs to do."

"No no." he beamed, "I will get working for you perfectly."

"In my budget?"

"Yes." he blinked.

She let out a quick sigh and turned to walk back the way they'd come.

"Wait Human!"

She did not listen to him so he gave chase as best as he could with his short little Prilt legs. Much to his relief he didn't have far to go. She'd only gone back to the ship and was climbing into the cockpit. As she plopped down into the pilot's seat, whose leather had more cracks than she could count, she looked around at all of the controls. It took only a moment to find what she was looking for and with the flick of a switch the hum of the reactor began to echo throughout the cavernous facility.

"Hey! You crazy?" Stors shouted up at her but she didn't pay him any attention. Her hands flew over the controls as she checked the rocket's systems. Landing gear was damaged, that much she already knew. Starboard engine was showing a faulty coolant regulator, life support systems didn't even respond to query, magnetic grapple showed as jammed and the seals to both cargo compartments registered as faulty. She began to check other systems but with a flicker all of the buttons on the control panel died out and the hum of the reactor faded. Faust looked down at the anxious little Prilt with an expression of derision.

"Just out of fuel."

She spun in her seat to look down the cramped corridor that led to the sleeping compartment. The fire extinguisher and emergency kit were missing from the wall and two of the light fixtures were hanging down from the ceiling. From the floor of the warehouse Stors could see her rise from the seat and hunch over before going aft to inspect the compartment. She was gone for a couple of minutes before her blonde head popped up out of the cockpit.

"You like?"

Again she did not respond. He watched as she slid down the side of the craft and landed on the deck with a thud larger than he'd thought her small frame capable of producing.

"Okay Stors. We've got a few things to talk about."

He smiled, "We can go to office." he motioned back through the jungle of spare parts.

"Works with me. I want you to get nice and comfy because I'm going to spell out *exactly* what I'm expecting before I give you a cent. Got it?"

The smelly little alien nodded his head eagerly.

8\\

"Well. He handled that better than I would have expected." Ansul quipped to the doctor, now up and about and standing at the top of the loading ramp.

"Mr. Ansul he ripped a chair out of the floor and tossed it through one of my monitors."

"...yeah...well you *were* the one who insisted on having him come to med-bay to break the news to him."

"That was in case he needed a sedative."

Ansul looked off into the distance before turning back to the doctor, "Well judging by his reaction I'd say he probably did."

"I didn't see you volunteering to hold him down while I administered it Mr. Ansul." the doctor smiled.

The Martian let out a small laugh at that.

"You got me there Doc. I didn't particularly feel like getting flung into a bulkhead."

"That still leaves us with a problem however, as I don't think he's up to this mission in his current state."

Ansul looked down the ramp and out onto the landing platform. Tarsik was standing near its edge and pacing back and forth, huffing to himself like a fuming dragon.

Beyond him was the hustle and bustle of all manner of

traffic coming and going. It was frantic but more organized and somehow "polite" than they were used to seeing at most busy spaceports. Ansul's eyes dropped back to his captain. He knew that Faust suddenly leaving without a word had done much more than leave the captain in an unfavorable position; Emily was a friend, he felt betrayed. Were she to ever come back he wasn't sure the two of them could ever work out their differences now.

"I can't help but feel responsible for some of this." Ramus remarked.

"How do you mean?" the Martian's brow furrowed as he turned back to the doctor.

"Faust thinks that she got me killed...got Herschel killed. *That's* why she left."

"And what do you think she'll do now?"

"I'd like to think she'd find some sweet young man, settle down here on Tersis, and have a family life. My gut, however, tells me that she'll be back in space before the week is out. She's just like the captain...and that is part of the problem."

"Yeah, well speaking of problem what are we going to do about *that one*?" he pointed at Tarsik, still pacing aggressively.

The doctor smiled as he extended his hand to Ansul.

"What is it?"

"It's a dermal patch, I've loaded it with a fairly strong sedative. Just press it against his skin when you get the opportunity and he'll settle right down."

"Okay...just checking here...but he's not going to go to sleep on me right? He's not any good to me or the mission if he's passed out."

"No it shouldn't make him sleepy at all but he'll be feeling pretty good." he passed the patch over to the first officer. "Just peel the backing off them press it down firmly. It will melt within seconds so he won't even know that it was there."

Resorting to his usual humor Ansul smiled, "Should be fun, now I gotta figure out a reason to get touchy feely with my captain who's incredibly pissed off right now."

Just as he finished his statement he noticed the doctor looking off in the distance. He strained his hearing and figured out what it was that had drawn the human's attention. The police transport was nearing and was slowing down for landing.

"Well, guess that's my ride Doc." he patted the doctor on the bare skin of his arm with the hand with which he'd just accepted the dermal patch. Ramus looked down quickly and checked the spot. Nothing. He looked up and was greeted by the sight of Ansul grinning and holding up the patch in his other hand. The doctor waved him away dismissively. The Martian let out a laugh and walked down the ramp, approaching the captain gingerly.

"Hey Harry." he said sheepishly, "How you doin' there buddy?"

The look of "Jet-off before I do something I'm going to regret!" was all the convincing he needed to halt his line of questioning immediately.

As the transport got closer Tarsik finally stopped pacing and instead was content to do his fuming standing still. Ansul took up a spot next to him, on his left, and looked out at the city and the approaching craft. As slowly as he could manage he brought his two hands together and peeled the backing off of the patch. Then, as the transport's engines went from a roar to a thunder he slapped the patch into the back of the captain's neck as deftly as he could. Without saying a word Tarsik grabbed the offending hand and twisted Ansul's arm until the Martian was on his knees.

"What in the hell was that for?" he demanded over the engine sound.

"A bug...you had a bug on your neck I swear it!" was all that Ansul could manage.

9\\

"I fully understand that this space station is not a science outpost but there has to be *someone* who can give me answers." Deutron Cal snapped at the meek young woman who'd suddenly found herself as second in command of Aeolus Station. He'd have preferred to have his first officer in that position but Commander Kada was overseeing repairs aboard the *Prometheus*.

"I..." she hesitated, "I've gone through personnel files and everyone with any kind of experience, no matter how small, in astrophysics of cosmic phenomenon has been assigned to a makeshift laboratory we've set up on deck 17."

"Then can you patch me down to them right now please?"

She thought to explain to him that they'd only been at it for maybe an hour and that he should give them more time but changed her mind and did as she was asked. A robo-screen flew over to where Captain Cal was sitting near the back of the command center, biting his nails. It flickered to life and he could see two men, one facing the camera and another a few meters behind him working at a console.

"This is the commander, please tell me you've got some idea why we're getting these power fluctuations and error codes all across the station. The goddamned engineers are stumped, saying it must be some kind of natural..."

The man on the screen had not been looking directly into the camera but did so as Deutron Cal stopped talking.

"What is it sir?"

"Your...your uniform. The blue stripe is vertical instead of horizontal." Cal remarked, noting that the uniform of the other man in the background was the same.

The man looked down at his shirt and laughed, "Is there some reason that's strange Captain?"

"Yes, all IPH uniforms feature a horizontal blue stripe, that's been in the dress code for thirty..."

Right before his eyes he saw someone enter the door to the lab and in an instant her uniform changed from the standard type to one with a vertical stripe. Her hair also appeared to grow from shoulder length to mid-back and changed from light brown into auburn.

"Sir?" came the voice over the vid-wave, breaking Cal's bewildered stare.

"I...the..." he pointed at the woman who'd just entered. The man on the screen turned to look at her but Deutron Cal jumped up from his seat and walked over to the railing to yell down at his new second-in-command. "Give me personnel files, now!"

The terrified young officer ran to the nearest console and used the station's computer to pull up the dossiers on all three people in the laboratory. Light brown shoulder length hair...and the man he'd been talking to was supposed to be bald. Something very strange was going on inside the Crux.

10\\

"Could you stop that please?" the police sergeant Dimitri Pterov demanded.

Tarsik, slouched in his chair, turned to the man with a huge grin and gave a one-word response, "No." With that he went right back to activating and de-activating his portable force-shield. Ansul chuckled to himself as the click-and-hiss of the device turning on yet again made the officer grit his teeth.

"Don't worry, he should only be like this for a few more hours." he assured them jokingly.

Pterov quipped, "Drugging your captain before we set off for an important mission...just what I'd expect from a couple of Servicemen."

"Hey!" Tarsik yelled as he clumsily kicked the back of Pterov's seat. "You watch your mouth...and Ansul?"

"Yes?"

"Remind me to punch you in the face when we get back to the ship okay? Real hard too."

The captain's speech was heavily slurred so Ansul could only hope that Harry would forget all about the whole drugging thing by the time they got back to Tersis and the *Honshu*.

"By the way, why's it take so damned long to get to that outpost anyway?" Tarsik had apparently lost the ability to control the volume of his own voice, either that or he just didn't care. The cockpit of the police cruiser was about half the size of the *Honshu*'s and was more long than it was wide so he sounded especially loud in the tight confines.

"Casidae law forbids use of NC while in-system. Besides, our cruisers are sub-light only." one of the men, this one sitting across from Ansul, explained.

"Well that's just stupid." the captain blurted out.

Ansul tried to ignore him and start an actual conversation. "I've been meaning to ask about that. Why does this system have such strict restrictions for the use of NC travel? I've never been anywhere that required rockets to drop to normal space so far out."

"Brecklin Incident." Pterov shouted back from the co-pilot's seat.

"Brecklin Incident?" Ansul asked the man who was across from him.

'Yeah, about a hundred and fifty years back a ship miscalculated and dropped out of NC-space only a kilometer or so above an outpost on Tersis' smallest moon. She impacted with about 600 gigatons of force. It was so powerful it changed the moon's orbit and sent it spiraling in toward the planet."

"That's incredible." Ansul said, shocked, "Obviously you stopped it though?"

"Yep. Took a worldwide calamity to get all of the politicians to stop bickering and work together. It was a huge public works project building the rockets we needed to put it back into its proper orbit. Scared the hell out of everyone so they passed a law preventing any NC travel in-system."

"And also unified the planet? I've never seen such a clean and well organized world before."

"That's right, and we're proud to help keep it that way." Pterov commented from the front.

Both Ansul and Tarsik knew how dangerous it was to mix NC drives and gravity wells. Back in the old days it was nothing for rockets to hit FTL shortly after breaking atmo but there'd been so many accidents. Still, there were careless captains out there who took risks and did crazy things like that. They'd seen it first-hand on many occasions. Tarsik followed proper procedure and though he'd typically okay an in-system transit if it was legal he always made sure they were well clear of any large bodies and that the calculations had been checked and double-checked.

"So. How long until we reach the outpost?"

"Nine hours sixteen minutes." the pilot called back to the Martian.

"Okay...I'm going to take a nap."

"Hey, we should sing a song!" Tarsik raised his hands and tried beckoned to everyone else.

"Or maybe not." Ansul said, exasperated.

11\\

Sitting in the cockpit of her new ship, which she had dubbed the *Feather* due to its relatively small mass next to the *Honshu*'s bulk, Emily Faust found that where she *should* have been filled with overwhelming joy there was instead a feeling of unease. It was not the way she *wanted* it to feel. Purchasing her own ship was something she had dreamed about for years. Going through the check-list for that first flight was supposed to be absolutely magical yet that was not what she felt. Guilt was the word of the day. She was experiencing guilt for leaving her crew, for causing the death of Herschel, and for disappointing her mentor.

"You ready to go, yes?" Stors called out over the telewave.

Faust leaned her pretty face over to peer out of the starboard-side glass so that she could see the little Prilt. He was standing on a makeshift launch pad, one that he had apparently built from the scrap in his warehouse. It wasn't new, as there were scorch marks on it indicating that it had been used before. That gave Emily a slight bit of hope that the crude facilities were up to the task.

Stors' dark little face, flat and wrinkled with large eyes, looked up at her and cracked a smile. He gave her a quick thumbs-up; a human gesture that had found its way into the repertoire of every species that was gifted with thumbs. She gave a quick one of her own before disappearing from the window and running the last of her checks. Despite never having even seen an F-Type intra-stellar transport before her hands danced across the control panel like she'd piloted it her entire life.

"I'm showing green across the board Control." she called out, then instantly felt silly for referring to one smelly little Prilt standing on a rudimentary launch pad as "Control".

"Good. Disconnecting from main power supply." he called out

A moment later, as Stors pulled the cables free of the *Feather*'s power ports Faust watched as the battery reserve indicators briefly dipped and then rose back to nominal levels exactly as they should as the ship switched over to purely internal power.

"Reactor functioning at 100%." she called out through her headset.

"Good...good. Backing away to safe distance. Your flight plan is filed and you are go for lift in 10 seconds. Good luck *Feather*."

Emily flicked a switch on the console that began a 10 second timer but, as an extra precaution, still turned to look out of the window to see that the shuffling little alien had cleared the pad before she finally engaged her engines.

Unlike most traditional rockets the *Feather* had some pretty impressive nega-grav generators that would lift her from the deck in a horizontal fashion before tilting 90 degrees toward the sky and allowing the main engines to power her into orbit. It was an ingenious system. It allowed the ship to make quicker and less punishing intra-atmospheric jaunts since it didn't have to use its neutron rockets just to get it aloft.

This trip, however, was into orbit to see what the *Feather* could do so after allowing her to slowly lift about five meters off of the ground under the power of her negagrav Faust slapped the switch which would orient her into vertical ascent position. As the nose of the craft raised Faust lost sight of the Casidaen star, slowly coming up over the horizon to the west, but then caught sight of Casadon, a nearby white dwarf star, in the dark of the early dawn sky.

"Emily how are your power levels?"

"Holding steady. Green across the board."

The mere fact that the little Prilt had bothered to ask again worried the pilot, but the fact that he'd addressed her in the familiar for the first time since they'd met made her think that perhaps it was simply friendly concern. She had to admit that Stors was about as amicable of a Prilt as she'd ever met, if that was even possible.

"Control, I am engaging engines."

With that she slammed the thrust control full-forward. She had every intention of truly putting the little ship through its paces.

A small part of her expected the refurbished old rustheap to flame out and coming crashing down to the launch pad. Maybe it was her way of wanting to admit to herself that she'd made a mistake in leaving the *Honshu*. The little ship, however, did not disappoint. With a tremendous roar, many orders of magnitude louder than that of larger rockets, the *Feather* blasted off.

Stors, ducked behind a piece of power conduit that he'd fashioned into a makeshift blast shield and cackled a raspy little Prilt laugh as nuts, bolts, and other loose debris pummeled his shelter.

There was no helping it, Faust felt her lips crack into a smile so goofy she'd not have wanted anyone else to have seen it. In an instant she felt that magic that she'd always anticipated. She was a little girl behind the controls of Daddy's ship for the first time all over again. While the *Feather* had nowhere near the total power the *Honshu* possessed it also weighed a hell of a lot less! Making orbit did not take long. The faint dark blue of the morning sky parted in seconds to reveal the magnificent clarity of space. Emily was still grinning widely as she cut thrust.

"Wooo!" she let herself belt out, all alone in the cockpit.

It was then that she noticed her butt beginning to float free of the seat and forgot that her new ship didn't have automatic activation of the grav-net. The quick press of a glowing red button that depicted a flat plane and some downward facing arrows turned the system on. It cycled orange as it charged and then green, at which time Faust could feel gravity pull her back into her seat. Being a primarily short-range craft the *Feather*'s grav net only produced 1/2G of force but it was more than enough for walking around or sitting in a chair.

"Okay, so she can rip your face off...time to see if she can actually do something useful." the pilot muttered to herself as she pressed a few buttons, scanning for the transit-module that Stors had launched into orbit with the help of a DX re-usable rocket.

"There she is." Faust whispered to herself after locating the module on scanners and then visually making out the faint glint of the metallic body against the blackness of space.

Most pilots would have simply plotted an intercept course and allowed the auto-pilot to slowly maneuver the ship into position but Emily Faust was no ordinary pilot. She slammed the thrust control into full power and squealed in delight as the nimble little craft blasted forth like a bullet from the barrel of a gun. In mere seconds she was closing on the module. Performing what most would consider an unsafe maneuver she cut power as she turned sharply and allowed inertia to carry her into an outer-space power-slide. The ship's little maneuvering thrusters tried desperately to slow her but accomplished little so another quick pulse of the throttle was required to cancel some of her backwards momentum. After that it was all thrusters as she guided the nose of the craft through the circular center of the transit-module. With a light touch that greatly contrasted her showboating of only moments earlier she guided the two craft into a gentle embrace and felt as the two made a positive lock. Lights on her console lit up green, indicating that the module was attached and reporting full functionality.

"Plotting course to edge of system." she said to herself then realized that there was no need to do so and was suddenly struck with a pang of loneliness. She shook it off and reassured herself that although the *Feather* had room for a small crew that she did not want anyone's life to ever be in her hands again.

12\\

"Well, if that wasn't the biggest waste of time I've ever taken part in." Tarsik muttered as he and Ansul stepped off of the police cruiser's ramp and back onto the landing pad where the *Honshu* was resting.

He was right. They'd squandered many vital hours flying all of the way out to Casidae VIIF. After taking the police shuttle down to the surface, one dominated by little more than gently rolling hills and grass for as far as the eye could see, they'd arrived at the little concrete bunker and abandoned landing pads of the old outpost. They'd found evidence that Essa had been there, but she'd left some time before they'd arrived. Von Braun was plenty clever enough to turn off the facility's scanner grid before her accomplices had arrived but she couldn't have known about the orbiting science probe that was studying the atmosphere and magnetic fields of the host planet. It had taken only a minute or two for one of the officers to patch into it from the outpost and pull up its logs. Not being designed to track ships the probe had little relevant data but enough to at least verify that she *had* indeed been met by a larger ship and that they'd activated NC only a short distance away from the planet.

This, of course, meant that she could now be anywhere in the galaxy but as luck would have it not an hour into their return trip to Tersis Minister Felize has waved in with news that the Casidae System perimeter scanner-net had intercepted a distress call coming from a ship identifying itself as the R.S. *Berydian*, an old Atlas Class rocket. What's more, the distress call had been detected only moments after the time the probe recorded the signature of an NC transit. It wasn't much, but it was the best they had to go on. Lying only 2.1 light-years distant from Casidae was the white dwarf Casadon and the minister had informed them that the *Berydian* was likely inside of that system's space when the call had been put out.

Tarsik had told the minister to cut short the repairs to the *Honshu* so that they could depart as soon as they'd arrived back at Tersis. As he strode toward his ship he was pleased to see that the fin damage had been mended and that everyone was aboard, presumably ready for lift. He thundered up the loading bay ramp followed closely by his first officer. Jones was standing at the top of the ramp.

"She's ready to lift sir. What's the word?"

"We're going to the white dwarf Casadon." he belted out as he tore past the crewman and headed for the lift.

"Aye sir." Jones said as he turned gave a sort of mock salute to Tarsik's back.

The captain was still none-too-happy about the fact that his pilot, his friend, had abandoned him and that he'd have to fly the mission himself. He said nothing as he and Ansul waited for the transport lift's doors to open up. When finally they did he strode quickly over to the pilot's seat and sat down, Ansul took up the station behind him, at the captain's console. It took the large man a few moments to adjust the seat to his liking before he started running his fingers over controls and performing pre-lift checks.

"*Honshu* to control, we are prepped for lift. Requesting clearance."

A moment later the tele-wave crackled to life, "Confirmed *Honshu*. We are showing pad as clear and your orbital vector unobstructed."

"Ansul, sit down." Tarsik commanded. The Martian quickly ran to one of the chairs at the back of the cockpit and strapped in. No sooner had he done so than the captain brought the engines up to power and slammed them into full-burn. He had none of the finesse that Faust possessed. He could certainly pilot a rocket, but his technique was less refined. He just applied thrust in the direction he wanted to go, and lots of it.

When they hit orbit Ansul unstrapped himself and made his way back to the captain's console

"Do you think you could pilot the ship...less angrily?" he quipped.

Ansul expected a sharp comeback but did not get one. Instead the captain sat in silence for a moment staring out of the front window.

"You're right Ansul. I've been letting my emotions get the best of me and that is not what a good captain does is it? Faust is gone, Herschel is dead. I've dealt with things like this before. I need to pull up my big-boy pants and stop acting like a child."

"Okay..." Ansul let slip, he hadn't meant to throw Harry into a sentimental reverie.

"From here on out I handle things the proper way...at least as proper as I'm capable of."

Ansul chuckled at that.

"Thank you for being my constant voice of reason old friend...even if you are a smart-ass."

"You're welcome." the Martian smiled.

Tarsik tapped a key to bring up communications with the planet. A few moments later the vid-screen made its typical static crackle as it began to glow and Minister Felize's image appeared on it.

"Captain Tarsik." he stated, "How may I help you?"

"I fully understand Casidae System law but I need to

request a special exemption in regards to in-system NC transit."

The minister nodded. "Agreed. If we wait for you to clear the system before transiting it may be too late to intercept the *Berydian*. Special permission granted. Just get well clear of the planet would you?"

"Absolutely." Tarsik nodded and with that cut communications. He plotted a course to clear the gravity well of Tersis then turned in his seat to face his first officer. "One more thing I wanted to bring up Ansul."

"What's that Harry?"

"If you ever drug me again I'm going to break your nose."

13\\

The Prilt merchant waited nervously as he watched Faust's craft descend from the sky and come to a slow descending hover over the launch pad. Her words, spoken only a few minutes before from orbit, still rang in his ears. "Stors you little hairball I'm going to kick your face in even flatter than it already is!"

The *Feather*'s FTL module had failed miserably and in a few moments the angry human would no-doubt be chasing him around his shop throwing tools and yelling curse words. Stors was no fool, he carried with him a 500,000 volt stun-stick just in case a client ever got a bit too rough. Still, he preferred to simply talk the problem out before it got to that point. He did, after all, have the ability to send up another rocket carrying a payload of repair robos which could get the drive working.

"Certainly not *that* one." he thought to himself, as he watched one of his maintenance inspection bots making its way across the launch pad, oblivious to the fact that it was about to be squashed by a landing F-Type. Luckily for the little machine, however, the ship's nega-grav field caught it in such a fashion that it simply tossed it about five meters where it landed on its side. It was MI3, that little robo had always been a bit quirky since the day he'd bought it off of a crew of Mercadian junkers along with the five other MI units he had on staff. The sound it had made, akin to a scream, as it had been flung through the air nearly made Stors chuckle.

As he watched the ship's landing struts begin to descend from the fuselage he ambled over and turned the little bot right-side-up. A moment later the clang of metal upon metal signified that the *Feather* had made contact with the launch pad. The gold-tinted cockpit glass flung open faster than the little Prilt had thought possible and a furious looking Emily Faust jumped out of her seat and slid along the hull to the deck, completely ignoring the hand and foot holds that were there explicitly for climbing into and out of the cockpit.

"I should have known better than to trust a greasy little pug like you!" she immediately regretted the racial slur but was so angry she kept charging right toward him. She nearly tripped as MI3 wandered directly into her path but she paid him little attention save for a swift kick which sent him flying into a pile of discarded power cells. As she approached him Stors went for the stun-stick, just in case. Faust noticed what he was reaching for and halted in her tracks. Her facial expression instantly melted from one of intense anger to one of genuine remorse.

"I'm so sorry Stors. I'm letting my previous experience with another member of your species cloud my judgment. That's the wrong thing to do." she then pointed at his belt, his hand tightly grasping the weapon, "You can put away the stun-stick. I'm not going to kick you."

She attempted a half-hearted smile and watched as the Prilt slowly came out of his defensive posture.

"You *are* going to get that module working though, otherwise we're going to have big problems. You got that?"

He nodded his nearly neckless little head, "Will make good on promises, you have my word. Will prep repair robos to go into space and fix right away. You give me coordinates of module, yes?"

"Get your rocket ready and I'll download them from the ship's data-tapes."

"Yes." he smiled.

She rubbed his little head as he walked past. She immediately regretted it. Not only was it likely degrading to the poor little man but now her hand also smelled of oil and all manner of other mechanical fluids.

14\\

Casadon was a white dwarf, the remnant of a sun-like star that had long-since collapsed into itself. It no longer produced energy by means of nuclear fusion but instead was simply radiating off the heat that remained in its core. What little information Tarsik could pull up on the dwarf star via the tele-net said that it was about one billion years into that particular phase of its life cycle and that there was no official governing body in the system. Minister Felize's records, which had been transmitted before the *Honshu* engaged NC, seemed to indicate, however, that there was some activity there. Likely a remnant world or two, or perhaps a space station. The fact that it wasn't well documented was worrying. Typically any star system which had activity, but no governing body, tended to attract to smugglers, pirates, and all sorts of unsavory characters.

If the area had at least been charted the *Honshu* would be able to drop into normal space somewhere near the hub of activity but since not even the Casidaens, who were either too self-important or too afraid to have explored the white dwarf system, had ever charted it they were forced to drop out quite a distance from the stellar remnant. Tarsik had no desire to end up inside the atmosphere of an uncharted gas giant or in a dense cometary belt.

"Well, that's a little odd." Ansul remarked as he looked up from the captain's console.

"Care to elaborate?" Tarsik replied.

"The ship's scanners are picking up one planet but nothing else. Certainly nothing putting out any kind of emissions that's for sure."

"No ships?"

"Not at the moment."

"What about the planet, biosphere?"

Ansul tapped a few keys, "It's hard to get specifics from this far out but it does look that way. Nitrogen-based atmosphere with a decent bit of oxygen and carbon dioxide with traces of methane. Looks pretty dry though."

"So no beaches filled with gorgeous alien women in skimpy bathing suits I presume?"

"Haha, were that the case maybe the Casidaens would have taken the time to investigate."

"So then a smuggler's hole, just as I'd feared."

"Smuggler's hole?" Crewman Jones asked. He had joined them in the cockpit and was manning the junior pilot's operations console.

"Service jargon for places so unappealing that nobody would ever want to settle it on purpose. They're usually little rocks in the middle of nowhere with barely breathable atmospheres that smugglers use as safe havens for black market trading. Places like this have no police presence, so where better?"

He nodded at the captain's response. "So the type of place where we can expect trouble?"

"You bet your ass." Ansul chimed in.

"What's wrong Jones, getting antsy? It's been like a week since you got to shoot somebody right?" Tarsik chuckled.

"Just saying...you might need somebody to watch your back."

"And that's why you and Fizril will be accompanying

Ansul and I when we leave the ship to go and find some answers. Von Braun's ship wasn't at the coordinates of the distress call...she's down there somewhere."

"How long until we reach orbit?" Ansul asked.

It felt strange for Tarsik to be the one answering that question, usually he was the one asking it. "Four hours, seventeen minutes. I'm going to put her on auto-pilot, who wants to grab a quick bite in the mess?"

"Ooh, yeah. I heard that Chef is doing Tersian Calamari."

"Alien squid, fantastic." Tarsik quipped as he entered commands into the ship's auto-pilot.

"You don't hear Jones over there complaining."

"That's because I'm not hungry. I'll grab a ration before we disembark." he grunted. Being ex-military he'd had to eat a lot of disgusting things in his life to survive but secretly he was quite a finicky eater and preferred field rations to half of the crazy stuff that Chef Grimmick cooked up.

"Oh well, you're loss...I hope." Ansul said as he slapped Jones on the arm, "Keep an eye on things up here would you?"

Jones nodded and watched as the two officers got into the transport lift. As the doors whirred closed he turned his gaze to the little dim star in the distance. He got up from his chair and walked over to sit in the pilot's seat. What a strange little object, long dead, yet it will continue to pour out energy for billions of years.

Before mankind had spread its wings and stretched out amongst the stars it had always been presumed that white dwarfs were incapable of supporting planets which were habitable. During their expansion phase, when their outer atmospheres had grown to enormous proportions and slowly sloughed off, it was believed that any planets in the inner system would be burned to a cinder or broken up completely. Reality has a way of surprising you, however, and many worlds had been discovered orbiting such stars.

Very seldom did they have any kind of complex ecosystem though. More often than not a few surviving microbes were the only things that had rebuilt the worlds into something that could support life, if only just. About one in every 25 or so white dwarfs had at least one of these planets. It was a peculiar quirk of the cosmos that no one had expected.

15\\

"Captain Tarsik?" the minister said, surprised as the Serviceman's image appeared on his screen. "What happened to your eye?" the minister had vid-waved the *Honshu* when it had suddenly reappeared at the edge of the system.

"Excuse me?" Tarsik grunted at the little man.

"Forgive me..." the adjunct security minister seemed perplexed, "but when we met earlier today you were not wearing an eye patch."

"Minister I've had this patch for over six years and we have never before met."

Felize had no idea how to respond. Surely he was not crazy. He had met with Captain Tarsik and his First Officer Ansul earlier in the day in the very office he now sat.

"Sir I can assure you..."

"Cut the crap Minister. Is this supposed to be some kind of game you're playing with me Tersian?"

"I can assure you not!"

"Something sure as hell is going on. I received acceptance confirmation of a contract that I have never even heard of. When I waved the asshole in charge at

Aeolus Station he informed me that my ship was already en route to Tersis. Interesting, since we only just arrived and have never been anywhere near that station since its construction. So please, cut the shit and tell me what the space-blasted hell is going on here!"

"Captain I...I don't know what to tell you. I was informed of your contract to hunt down the fugitive Essa Von Braun, former commander of Aeolus Station, and when you arrived in-system we met in my office." he gestured to the space around himself though it was not visible on the screen, "You and your First Officer, Ansul."

Tarsik squinted, deep in thought. "Minister I have never heard of anyone named Ansul in my life."

The two sat in silence for a moment.

"Captain Tarsik I really do not understand. You were here, you had no eye patch, you had a Martian with you, and you recently departed to investigate the white dwarf Casadon."

"Sir Casadon is only 2.8 light years distant. We could be there in no time." Pilot Jones chimed in.

"Pilot Faust?!" came the voice over the vid-wave.

She turned the screen to face her and spoke into it, "I *was* Emily Faust, Emily Jones now. What of it?"

"My records indicate that Pilot Faust is...was...the only female member of your crew but that she departed your ship shortly after it arrived. The last information I have on her shows that she filed a flight plan in a newly registered Casidaen F-Type that returned to Tersis just a few hours ago."

Tarsik's head hurt. Was there really a counterfeit *Honshu* out there with a crew pretending to be his?

"So these people were obviously *not* me or my crew, seeing as how we're here now, but whoever they were you certainly were keeping a tight watch on them."

"Captain I'm just as confused as you. Their personal idents as well as that of the ship checked out. Personnel records on Captain Harridor Tarsik did not indicate any eye injury and everything I've gotten from the service lists the R.S. *Honshu* as being blue in color, not green. I'm sorry Captain but at this point you seem more of an anomaly than the other ship."

"Seriously?" Jones spoke up, "You've got scopes trained on our ship to see what *color* it is?!"

The minister nodded. "Absolutely. You'll find that security in the Casidae system is top notch."

"So you just spy on everyone in your space do you? Sorry, but it doesn't sound like the kind of place for me." Jones spat out.

Tarsik made a gesture at her that told her to shut it.

"Regardless Minister we *are* here. We'd like your help in sorting this matter out."

"I'm afraid I can't do that Captain. As far as I know you could be imposters and allies of the fugitive Essa Von Braun. I can't risk sharing any more information with you than I've already foolishly provided. If you'd like to set down we can have an in-person meeting and wave up someone from the Service to help sort all of this out."

"I don't think so. We'll be off to Casadon to investigate this matter ourselves. Have a good day Minister."

He went to press the button to cut communications but the minister spoke up, "I'm afraid I'm going to have to insist Captain."

"Pardon?"

The man on the screen was punching buttons on his desk, "I'm clearing a pad for you and sending the coordinates. Under my authority as adjunct security minister of the Casidae system I am hereby ordering you to put down immediately."

"Sir, three police cruisers on an intercept course." Pilot Jones called out.

"Felize you son of a bitch, what's the meaning of this?"

"Please cooperate Captain, I'd really hate to see anything happen to you or your ship."

With that the screen went blank. Back inside of

Minister Felize's office his display lowered itself back into his desk. He spoke softly to himself as he sat motionless, "Oh my dear Captain Tarsik, whatever have you done to space and time?."

The little bot that had just flown down from the ceiling with a steaming hot cup of coffee beeped an acknowledgment at his words before flying away.

16\\

"A little rough eh Harry?"

Tarsik was not amused at Ansul's comment on his lack of finesse in landing the ship. "We're down in one piece aren't we? You wanna try?"

"No thank you." Ansul shook his head. "So what's the plan, just burst into the place and start demanding answers?"

"Nobody can say you don't understand me Ansul." he said to his first officer as he unbuckled from the pilot's seat and stood up. He pointed to the lift, signaling for the Martian to go first.

They'd set down about a kilometer from the largest settlement they could find on the odd little planet-that-shouldn't-be. Even if there were no active scanners at the settlement they'd no doubt seen the mighty blue rocket descending from the heavens. The size of the welcoming party would signal just how hostile of a reception they were likely to get in such a place. Down in the loading bay the two spacers geared up as did Jones and Fizril. Walking out onto the surface of the harsh world it was easy to see why no one save for smugglers would want to live there. Fine grained dust stirred up constantly in the thin atmosphere and just over the horizon hung the unbelievably bright specter that was the white dwarf Casadon. In stellar terms it may not have been the biggest or brightest of objects but the little world's extremely close orbit made it appear as a behemoth in the sky. It was warm, too warm to be comfortable, but having just spent some time on cretaceous-era Earth the lack of humidity made it feel comparatively mild. The four men trudged through the shifting sand, so fine that each step kicked up more of it into their faces, forcing them to tie handkerchiefs over their mouths and noses. As they came over the last dune and began to be able to make out the shapes of buildings through the haze of fine dust that seemed to glow in the intense light of the white dwarf they were amazed to see that no one had come out to meet them.

"Hmm. Maybe they're not hostile." Ansul smiled.

"Or they are so secure in their numbers that they do not fear us." Fizril said glumly.

"It could very well just be a waypoint for smugglers and shady travelers, nothing too organized. We may just be able to blend in if we avoid questions as much as possible." Tarsik had demanded that everyone wear their personal dress, no need to show up in Service uniforms or expedition gear and spook the locals. Smugglers didn't necessarily have anything against the Service but any pirates that might be around certainly would. He turned to his men, "Ansul, by my side as usual. Fizril, you're my eyes and ears, stay sharp. Jones, if anyone so much as *reaches* for a gun...burn 'em to the ground."

"Definitely" the crewman responded. Fizril and Ansul just nodded.

Their early assertion quickly proved to be incorrect. Closing in on the collection of buildings, which had been several hundred meters from their position atop the dunes, they began to be able to discern a few shapes milling about in the dust. Most of them hurried from building to building, holding tattered remnants of cloth over their faces as they did so. One figure stood out.

"Slizarian." the captain muttered to himself, eyes locking on the beast. Nearly as tall as Fizril but likely twice his girth the reptilian stood at the break between two structures that led to what looked to be a sort of main thoroughfare. His arms were crossed, his stance wide, no attempt made to cover his face from the elements.

"Nictitating membrane", Tarsik thought. Ganda IV was an arid world with intense sandstorms, the creature's people had evolved transparent eyelids that could easily protect their vision against howling dust. He remembered having read something about their sinus structure being able to filter out much of the airborne debris as well. This creature, who it was becoming more obvious by the moment had come out to greet them, was far more suited to this environment than any of the men from the *Honshu*.

"Gasto fredrax." the reptilian spoke in a loud and booming voice as they drew near. A cursory glance revealed that none of the other natives were moving about any longer. Had they been scurrying about seeking shelter before an inevitable firefight? Some scene out of a film about the ancient American west?

"I'm sorry," the captain shouted over the howl of the wind, "I can't understand you."

"Shandrit translator couspan interference asto gris dust storm."

The words were broken but the four men gathered the gist of what the alien had said. Much to their surprise the large creature turned and waved for them to follow. The captain glanced back at his men and with a quick shrug motioned for them to do as they'd been told. He let them walk past him, caught sight of Jones surveying the rooftops as they went. As they made their way down the street, everything in sight covered in a heavy layer of fine near-white dust, not a soul seemed to be stirring. All doors closed, all shutters drawn. He thought he glimpsed a few pair of eyes staring out from between the slats of some of them but it could have simply been his imagination.

After what had amounted to likely less than two or three minutes of walking they approached a building with a doorway with considerably more height than those around it. Along one of the pillars that flanked it was attached a neon sign, "The Rusty Rocket". Bright red in color it flickered on and off, likely due to the same effects that had rendered their translators nearly useless. At the entrance the Slizarian stopped and motioned for them to enter. His men glanced back at him but Tarsik motioned for them to enter.

The large alien held out his arm for the captain to enter but he declined, instead suggesting that he would follow. The Slizarian hesitated but then agreed. Tarsik, of course, had his spiral-ray drawn under his cloak and pointed right at the large creature's back. Jones no doubt had his sidearm drawn under his as well. Ansul probably had his hand on his kasik-blade, Fizril ready to bare claws at a moment's notice.

As the outer door closed behind them with a hiss, silencing the sound of rushing wind outside, the men became aware that they were standing in what was essentially an airlock, or at very least a *dustlock*. "It made sense." the captain thought. He'd seen it on arid worlds before. No sense in letting the interior of your establishment become covered in dust in such quantities that it could never actually be cleaned. Such a modification also helped hold in moisture and kept the drinks of customers from evaporating away as they sat at the bar. Still, such a setup did not come cheap. A tavern it might be, but the Rusty Rocket was making money in more ways than serving drinks to wayward smugglers and pirates.

"I am Grogg, welcome." the Slizarian croaked in his peculiarly deep, almost frog-like, voice.

"Captain Brigsby." Tarsik lied. "These are my men, Crewmen Hennick and Ferran, and my First Mate Pargo."

Grogg nodded in acknowledgment at each man in turn. Rather polite for a smuggler, or whatever he was.

"I can't help but notice that the translators seem to be working just fine now."

"An effect of the dust storms Captain. They generate enough static electricity to cause issues with much of our technology."

Not wanting the conversation to turn to exactly who they were or what their business was Tarsik asked, "May we enter? My men and I are quite parched after our walk."

"Indeed." Grogg spoke in a calm manner, "Which raises a question. Why did you choose to set down so far from town when we have landing pads on the outskirts?"

"That settles it, they'd definitely tracked us as we landed." Tarsik thought to himself, then spoke to his new host, "You must forgive us, we did not intend to arouse suspicions...but we're new to this sector of space and did not wish to barge in and cause a stir. We can identify with being wary of strangers, so sure your suspicion is understandable."

"Hmmph." Grogg grunted then slapped a large green button on the sandstone wall that he was standing near. The inner door, a roughly oval-shaped one made out of an ornate metal and glass lattice slid open at the middle to reveal a contrastingly pedestrian establishment. He gave a head motion indicating that the rocket-men were free to enter.

As they stepped over the threshold each and every one of them scanned the area thoroughly. To the left an open room some twelve by twelve meters and dotted with many simple wooden tables. One large window sat at its farthest end and let in most of the light in the establishment. Only two of the tables were occupied, one with a single human man of advanced age who wore an eye patch, the other with two more humans of about middle-age and appearing to be of the rough-and-tumble variety. They looked up carefully, examining the strangers but being cautious as they did so. To the right, the bar, about five meters in length was populated by a few empty bar stools and had a surface made from what appeared to be part of a hull panel from an old intra-stellar tug. It had been covered in bric-a-brac from all over the galaxies and then sealed with a thick layer of urethane. Approaching it they pulled out stools for themselves and Tarsik glanced over the items embedded deeply in the sealant. A service badge...no two of them...countless system police badges, some he recognized, some he did not.

"Definitely pirates..." he thought to himself.

"Can I help you gentlemen?" the bartender, a thickly built man with a bald head and chin-strap beard, asked with a raspy voice that told all of them that he'd been a heavy clove-spice smoker his entire life. Another clue that pointed in the direction of pirates. It was well known that most of them liked to partake in the very addictive practice regularly and actively protected clove-spice smugglers to ensure their supply.

Tarsik pulled down the cloth he'd been using to cover his nose and mouth and locked eyes with the man. "I think that you can. First I'd like a round of kaska for me and my men."

The man smiled, though it thinly veiled his obvious contempt. He, Grogg and possibly the other men in the bar likely knew exactly who they were...or at least *what* they were. A fight was imminent but still the bartender did as asked and poured shots of kaska for all four men.

Tarsik glanced over at Jones, hoping the damned tool would be smart enough to not immediately throw back the deceptively powerful drink. He didn't. While the others were facing the bar Jones straddled the stool sideways, so as to keep an eye on the men at the tables.

"Secondly?" the barkeep asked.

The captain smiled, "Yes, secondly I'd like to know the location of a woman named Essa Von Braun. Something tells me that little escapes your attention on this rock and that if she is hereabouts you would know precisely where."

The man chuckled just a bit under his breath then looked up from the glass he had begun to clean. "I am going to assume that you noticed our little...trinkets laid into the bar." he sneered, "Bounty hunters and rogue police agents don't have a habit of surviving very long on Zanj."

Cute. They'd named their little rock.

"Well then, it's a good thing for us that we're neither of those things." Tarsik grinned sarcastically as he reached for his gun under his cloak.

The bartender paid him little attention as he turned to place the glass onto the shelf behind him before picking up another and taking his visibly filthy rag to it. After wiping it down, cloth squeaking against glass, he once again turned to the shelf. "Then that leaves but one possibility Captain, that you are Service and operating on a private contract. I also know that you're reaching for that weapon concealed deep within your layers of clothing. It'll do you no good."

Tarsik's eyes shot to the corners of the room, small black orbs that dotted each one of them told the confirmed the barkeep's warning.

"Inhibitor field." Tarsik chuckled softly, "Smart for this type of establishment. I give you credit."

The man behind the bar grasped for something in a nearby drawer, a metallic clink and then a gleam of metal as his hand rose, quicker than the captain had thought possible, to present a blade to his throat. Behind him he heard the grunt of wooden chairs against concrete floor as they slid back from their tables and the men at them rose to their feet. He heard the stirring of his own men as well but put out a low hand to steady them.

"Who are you?" the man with the blade demanded in his raspy tone, pressing it slightly harder into the captain's flesh.

"Someone who knows something that you don't." the

captain snickered.

"Oh?" he snapped, "What would that be? Because I think you and your men are about to be stripped naked and staked down in the desert for the dust storms to strip you to your bones."

The captain smiled then looked up, careful to not move his head, at the man who held the knife to his throat. "I'm a lot faster than I look."

In a lightning fast move he grabbed the man's wrist with his left hand and pulled it away from his neck, twisting it painfully as he did so. Without even looking over Ansul, who'd been sitting to his right, struck full force and broke the man's elbow. The barkeep screamed out in pain and dropped the blade to the bar where it stuck into the thick veneer of lacquer. Tarsik grabbed the shot glass of kaska in front of him and tossed it into the man's face, which provoked a blood curdling scream as the tremendously powerful drink instantly burned sensitive eyeballs.

"Inhibitor field!" Tarsik cried out, "Hand to hand!"

Jones and Fizril jumped into action, tossing their glasses of kaska into the eyes of the men who were approaching them from behind, as Tarsik jumped up from his stool and punched the barkeep in the nose, causing the man to stagger backwards.

Ansul spun to assist the other crewmen but could see that they were having no trouble with the two men who had been brave enough to attack. The third, the older man, chose instead to stand near the window and simply watch the proceedings.

Pulling his kasik-blade from its sheath Ansul followed Tarsik as he walked around the end of the bar. Being on a low gravity world such as Zanj the captain had little trouble lifting the barkeep off of his feet and slamming him back through the shelf full of dirty glasses and into a mirror which promptly shattered into jagged shards. Immediately the battered barkeep began to paw, with his still usable hand, at a pocket on his vest. As quick as he'd smashed the man's arm at the bar Ansul leapt forward and snatched his wrist to prevent him from going for another weapon.

"Captain!" he exclaimed, "Look at this."

Tarsik turned his attention down to the barkeep's wrist, which bore a familiar tattoo.

Both spacers were surprised. Smugglers were looked down upon, pirates were both feared and hated, but *no one* was as universally loathed as the small but very real Slavers' Guild. How anyone, in a day and age when automation is cheap and affordable, would prefer to steal the life of another sentient was beyond the understanding of any of the *Honshu*'s men.

"Slaver!" the captain roared, his eyes filled with rage. He fumed and leaned in until his massive body was pushing the man into the fragments of mirror glass whereupon a few of them audibly crunched as they dug into the man's back.

"Let me make this immensely clear. I kill pirates, hell I even kill smugglers...so I have *absolutely* no qualms about killing a slaver. In fact it would make my day to put one more of you in the grave. Tell me where Essa Von Braun is and I *might* consider only cutting that tattoo from your arm and breaking a few of your bones!"

"You're forgetting one thing." the slaver smiled, then motioned toward the front door with his head which was now running with blood which had begun to streak down behind his ears and pour from his broken nose.

"What?" Ansul laughed, "The big Slizarian?"

Until then the large alien had simply stood there, watching the scene unfold. Arms still crossed a wry smile came over his thin lips and he began to step forward. His footsteps were heavy, easily telling his immense weight even in the low gravity.

"Oh, did you not see Fizril?" Ansul scoffed then turned to look at the big cat who was dangling one of the patrons off of the ground by his wrists.

"This one is a slaver as well." Fizril said, nodding to the tattoo on the man's arm.

"Then why don't you give him a few punches to the gut there Fizril?" the captain remarked, never lifting his gaze from the barkeep.

"With pleasure." the crewman responded. The sound of several heavy blows followed.

"Grogg!" the barkeep yelled, "No matter what happens to me or the others rip these fools apart!"

"Ooh, bad answer." Ansul snapped before back-handing the bloodied slaver scum.

"Fizril?" the captain called over his shoulder, "You got this guy?"

"No problem." the cat smiled, then lifted the man he'd been holding over his head and tossed him down on top of a table which promptly shattered into pieces.

"You're man was waiting for us when we arrived..." Tarsik began, the sound of Fizril letting out a low growl and then jumping over several tables could be heard in the background, "...I know you know where Von Braun is. You're going to tell me where she is or I'm going to get *very inventive* with my methods of persuasion."

The barkeep spit in his face. Wrong move.

With all of his strength Tarsik cocked back his right fist and smashed it into the man's jaw so hard he was certain that he'd dislocated it as well as shoved his head back into yet more fragments of shattered mirror glass. The man let out a low moan but only smiled and attempted to look over the captain's shoulder.

"What? You want to see?" Tarsik remarked. "Okay, take a look."

As forcefully as he could he pulled the man from the shelves he was embedded in and tossed him onto the bar so that he could see Fizril and Grogg having it out. Ansul casually walked around the bar and with the butt of his gun smashed the man's hand as it reached in futility for the knife that had moments before been lodged into its surface.

"That's a bad boy Mr. Slaver." he said snarkily.

Tarsik walked up from behind and lifted the battered man's face, to give him a better view. Back-lit against the large window the two behemoths circled one another, roaring in aggression. Tarsik liked to think himself quite a formidable opponent but after having his clock thoroughly cleaned some years back by a Slizarian he found himself very glad to have the Antarian crewman along.

"Watch this." he said to the barkeep.

Grogg shifted on his feet and swung wide a powerful swipe, his large talons aimed for the agile cat's soft belly. Fizril deftly avoided the strike and used the opportunity to push the massive creature off-balance. With a ferocious yowl Fizril then lifted a clawed hand and sunk it into Grogg's flesh near where his short excuse for a neck met his back. The reptilian grunted in pain but seemed less affected than any of them had expected.

What's more, the crewman's claws seemed get stuck in the thick leather-like hide of the beast. Grogg looked down at the helpless arm and smiled. Had it not been for the quick reaction of Jones, who picked up a glass from a nearby table and slung it into the reptile's face, he likely would have broken Fizril's relatively dainty wrist with ease. The shattering of glass into his left eye, however, gave the cat just enough time to break free and drop to the ground, sweeping the heavy creature's feet out from under him. Grogg crashed to the floor, taking a nearby table with him as he grasped at it attempting to prevent his own fall.

"Watch what?" the beaten man on the bar scoffed, "Your big pussycat needing help to fight Grogg?"

Ansul whistled to himself as he pulled the knife free of the bar and thrust it down through the man's hand, nailing it to the lacquered surface.

"Ah!" the man screamed, "You son of a bitch!"

"Ansul!" Tarsik yelled at him. "Mind your manners.

There'll be plenty of time to gut this pig later."

The Martian just looked back at his captain and gave a grinning shrug.

Across the room Fizril had, sportingly, waited for his opponent to get to his feet.

"I am going to rip your spine out with my bare hands Antarian!"

"I invite you to try." Fizril sneered toothily.

The big Slizarian cocked back onto his right foot in a fighting stance. Fizril did likewise and prepared himself for the attack.

"Stop playing and finish this please." Tarsik ordered. The flick of the Antarian's ear served as an acknowledgment but allowed him to keep his gaze locked on his enemy. Grogg roared heartily and lunged forward. Fizril deftly jumped to the side and, using Grogg's own weight against him, slammed his knee into the big beast's abdomen as hard as he could, then followed with a quick right to the base of the creature's skull. Grogg crashed to the floor so hard that for a moment Tarsik thought that perhaps he was dead.

The low grumble which followed shortly, however, demonstrated that he was not. Pawing at one of the unbroken tables he pulled himself to his feet. No sooner had he done so than Fizril leapt at him full force, sending him careening backwards, stumbling through a minefield of chairs and tables. The cat may not have weighed even half what he did but the ferocity of the attack was more than enough to cause the ungainly Grogg to lose his balance.

He tried desperately to push the flailing cat, now in complete berserker mode, from his chest. With slash after slash Fizril tore at the relatively soft flesh of his chest and just before they crashed into the wall at the far end he cocked back his right hand and brought it forward with full force. A single powerful blow to Grogg's jugular brought the creature's thrashing to a quick end as he released Fizril and grasped at his throat. The crewman jumped back, immediately landing in a fighting pose.

Grogg stumbled forward, his eyes spinning in his head, and Fizril allowed him to do so. As he passed, seemingly no longer even aware of the Antarian he'd been locked in battle with, the crewman pulled the knife from his belt and with a single spin lodged it in between two vertebrae at the base of the Slizarian's spine. The body crashed through two tables, sending bits of smashed wood flying about the room.

As soon as the scene before them fell silent Tarsik pulled the knife from the barkeep's hand and yanked the man to his feet before tossing him hard onto the floor. The spacer knelt down in front of the slaver.

"Now let me explain what is about to happen. First, we're going to take our time cutting...or perhaps burning, those Slaver Guild tattoos from your arm and the arms of your friends...then we're going to have a nice long chat about Essa Von Braun."

17\\

"What great evil hath been brought upon us by the wickedness of the tribes?" the scribe's pen etched the words noisily onto the scroll.
This shadow that crosses the land, in the form of an avenging angel it does come.
Blotting out the sun by day it looms above our world.
Hath not our course been steady and true?
Perhaps, but what of the course of the other tribes?
Women and children fall to their knees, weep in the shadow of the worldshaper.
Men tremble, though dare not show it, hide it beneath their robes.
But what good is trembling, or weeping?
For if it is meant to be then Yadra shall strike us from this world as easily as a man snufts the embers of his fire.
But that is not his will.
His will is the coming of the redeemer, the foretold one Deliah, who shall remake Dathon for all time.

- translated from the Testament of the Prophet Joachim, year 0 B.R.

18\\

"I do not get paid enough for this shit Captain." the pilot snapped at her commander, half in anger, half in jest.

"Good job Emily." Tarsik said as he reached over his console and patted her on the shoulder.

Outside of the cockpit windows floated large rocks, asteroids, that would under normal circumstances be far too close for comfort. These were anything but normal circumstances. They'd been chased by police cruisers, and all for what? For being...themselves? None of it made a bit of sense.

"Keep a sharp eye. I don't want any of these things making a hole in my ship."

"Gotcha Cap'." she responded.

Pilot Jones was strapped tightly into her seat. They'd gone zero-G, killing virtually every system on the ship so as to keep themselves hidden for the three police cruisers who were, at that very moment, scanning the debris field for signs of them.

Captain Tarsik floated behind his console, holding onto it for stability. "Herschel?" he asked, looking at the dark-skinned young officer, "Can you give me some kind of number, *any* kind of number, on the probability of them finding us in here?"

The junior pilot ran through the switches and dials on his controls deftly, his display screen changing several times, its light one of the only things illuminating the dim cabin. "If I really had to make a guess..."

"Yes Herschel, you *do* really have to make a guess. Spit it out."

"Seventy-five percent or so that we go unnoticed."

"That's not *too* bad." the captain thought to himself. His eyes caught something out of the window, he tensed.

"Clench up gentlemen." Pilot Jones said softly, "Police Cruiser dead ahead."

The captain saw Herschel flick a few controls and nearly shouted at him not to activate any of the ship's systems but before he could say anything the junior pilot spoke up, "Casidaen System Police Cruiser 83, passive scanners pick her up at 2.7 kilometers off the port bow."

"Too close..." Tarsik whispered.

"We've got 'em dead-to-rights Captain." Emily said over her shoulder, "We could take out their sensors and engines before they knew what hit them."

"Absolutely not Pilot." still speaking in a soft voice, sound waves didn't travel in space but if the cruiser's laser scanner happened to pass over their hull it'd pick up any reverberations from inside, "We fire on a system police ship and not only are our careers over but we'll be hunted until the day we die. Even pirates aren't typically that stupid."

He couldn't see her expression but it was one of utter shame. She was surprised at herself for even suggesting it.

Tarsik detected something with his eyes, very faint, but it was definitely there. Something had changed with the police cruiser.

"Herschel?" he queried.

"On it." apparently he had seen the same thing, "Sensor probes, that's the best I can tell with the passive scanners sir. Looks like they've launched a cloud of them."

"Fantastic, they'll be on us in no time." the captain grumbled, "Faust...err Jones I'm readying the ship's systems for return to full power. If that cruiser so much as glances in our direction I want us gone, got it?"

"Yes sir." she smiled wickedly. The girl that'd been a goody-two-shoes only a few weeks before was now apparently beginning to have some of her husband's rebellious attitude rub off on her. Running from the cruisers only minutes before had been surprisingly exhilarating. She could still feel the rush of adrenaline surging through her body and she liked it.

"Naughty naughty Emily." she thought to herself, "Maybe you should have been a smuggler, or hell even a pirate." then she mused, "No, thrills are one thing but I'm not that hateful. I could hurt people just for the fun of it like pirates are known to do."

Herschel's console, set to mute, did not emit a sound but the flashing of a red indicator drew the attention of everyone in the cockpit. The captain looked at him questioningly, his hands poised over the switch that would kick the *Honshu*'s systems back into full power.

"It's not the police cruiser." Herschel said softly, surprise apparent on his youthful face even in the dimly lit cabin. "Picking up another craft. Casidaen F-Type, one-hundred-fifty-thousand kilometers to port. It seems to be rather interested in what's going on here, she's scanning the cruisers."

"That's pretty audacious." Tarsik thought to himself, "Could it be? The Minister had said that the imposter Faust had purchased one of those old relics. Was she searching for her crewmates?"

"Captain, head's up." Faust called out.

Peering out of the front window he saw what she was referring to. One of the probes was closing on their position rapidly. It didn't look like it was going to intercept, but it would be a close pass.

"Think happy thoughts." he whispered to the others as

it zipped by them. Collectively they let out a sigh once it was safely out of sight behind them. Their calm was short lived, however, as only seconds later an indicator on Tarsik's panel lit up.

"Launch detected from the cruiser, low-yield atomic by the signature. They mean to flush us out!" his hands flew over the controls, "Going to full power. Pilot give me everything you've got, evade that thing!"

"It's gonna be close Captain!" she called out as she slammed the engines to maximum and the rocket lurched forward with tremendous force. Tarsik barely managed to keep his grip on his console. The gravity kicking back in helped, but only a little.

"Fifteen seconds to impact..." Herschel called out.

Pilot Jones aimed the ship's bow straight for one of the larger asteroids between them and the police cruiser.

"What in the space-blasted hell is she doing?" Tarsik thought to himself, but trusted in her abilities and reasoning.

"We're going to impact the surface ma'am!" Herschel cried out.

"Three...two...one..." Jones mumbled to herself. When it seemed as though they would be smashed into millions of pieces against the hard surface of the gigantic space rock she banked hard, harder than the captain had thought the old ship was capable of. A second or two later the the ship shook and flashing lights lit up all over the cabin. That had been close.

"Banking away. Shall we make a run for the outer system Captain?"

Astonished at what she'd just pulled off it took Tarsik a moment to compose himself, "No. That's a negative Pilot, set an intercept course for that F-Type that Herschel detected."

"Sir?" came her response.

"We can outrun the cruisers until we get there can't we?"

"Absolutely. We've got them beat hands-down, in the sprint at least, but where does that get us? How's an old rock-hopper going to help?"

"I just put my trust in you Pilot." he glanced over at Herschel, noticed the look of complete confusion on the man's face, "She acted on instinct, knew that the atomic had been set to detonate at range so as to cripple us with the EMP and not to vaporize us...she put the asteroid between us and the torpedo gambling that it'd come within range and go up while we were in the asteroid's shadow, safe from the electromagnetic wave.

He turned back to Jones, "For the quick thinking I can't commend you enough Pilot, but I'm going to have to ask you to simply trust *me* now. It's either that or I can remind you that this is my ship and that I just gave a direct order." he smiled.

19\\

"I will go in sir." Fizril gave a slight bow to the captain.

"While I'm sure your night-vision has mine beat by several orders of magnitude I have some doubts that it even comes close to competing with that of a Martian." Tarsik put his hand on Fizril's shoulder, "I appreciate the selflessness Crewman but Ansul should have this covered. Don't you Ansul?"

"Oh yeah." the Martian beamed a large grin as he pulled his proton pistol from its holster and spun it around several times in his hand before lifting it to his lips and blowing on the barrel. Had his dark goggles not been covering his eyes Tarsik was certain that he'd have seen a wink from the quirky Martian.

"Don't get too cocky Ansul," he reminded, "she's a slippery one and not afraid to leave bodies in her wake."

"No worries Captain, I've got no intention of getting caught in the sights of that damnable KA7Z she carries. Don't want you and the doctor boo-hooing over my deathbed as I meet a slow and agonizing end."

"Just pop the goddamned lock." Tarsik chuckled.

"Roger Cap." Ansul said, looking over at his commander with a silly grin, the near-blackout goggles lending even more humor to his already amusing appearance.

After threatening to let Fizril loose on the barkeep the man had finally spilled the beans and revealed that he did, in fact, know where Essa Von Braun was hiding. It was near a launch pad situated at the opposite end of the town from where the *Honshu* men had entered. She was apparently only planning on passing through. Plans that Tarsik was only too happy to disrupt. She'd seen them approaching however and had sent a couple of men, one Zulian and one human, to stop them. Their ambitions had been high but their marksmanship had been atrocious. Jones had taken both of them out so quickly that his friends hadn't even had a chance to draw their weapons. Too bad, the captain had no qualms about disintegrating slavers. In fact he had a mind to turn the *Honshu*'s atomic torpedoes on the whole nest of them after they broke orbit. He'd have to think more on it.

During the remarkably brief firefight they'd seen Von Braun bolt for the holding tanks not far from the launch pad. There were at least five dozen of them, many of them interconnected. H2O faded paint denoted, they were water tanks, or at least they *had* been at one time. They all sounded hollow and many of them had small rust holes in their metal. After a brief sweep of the area it was apparent that the cunning woman had hidden inside some of the empty ones so Ansul, being the one with the best natural ability to see in low light, had been chosen to go in after her.

Jones and Fizril grasped firmly onto the rusted wheel-lock of one of the tanks' hatches and gave it a good tug. It failed to budge. Only after the captain added in his muscle did it finally give way. They peered inside carefully, it was lit ever so faintly by the white dwarf's starlight that penetrated through tiny holes in the tank's shell.

"Will you be able to see in there?" Tarsik asked his first officer.

"Should be no problem. She'll never know what hit her."

"Okay. We're going to seal this hatch behind you."

Ansul simply nodded as he stepped into the entrance. Fizril pushed the metal door closed and turned the wheel to seal it.

"You and you," the captain indicated the two crewmen, "I want you up on that ridge, and you up on that building. If you see her bolt for it you've got my permission to take her down, understood?"

"Aye sir." they chimed in unison.

Tarsik planned to stay on the ground, listen for any rustling sounds in the labyrinth of tanks and pipes that would indicate a struggle.

Inside the first tank, door shut behind him, Ansul removed the welding goggles that were essential for protecting his sensitive Martian eyes against the harsh light of Zanj's sun. He blinked a few times and his vision came into focus. Perfect. There was plenty of light to see but not so much as to blind him.

Silently he moved through the corroded old structure. It was some six or seven meters across and ahead he could make out the tube that connected it to the next tank. "Easily wider than 2 meters." he thought, "Good, I wont have to do any crawling in here."

His attention shifted to his tele-wave, still fastened to his belt. He reached for it and turned it off. No reason to let it betray him should it pick up some random signal. He moved carefully, slowing his breath consciously and taking note of the faint sound that his boots made against the metal of the floor. Here and there they would find a spot of metal that seemed to be more rusted through than others. He made a mental note to watch for such soft spots, as he had no desire to fall through.

Inside of the connecting pipe he found a valve, only slightly smaller than the 2 meter tube itself, which had luckily been left open and that he was easily capable of squeezing through. Inside the next tank it appeared exactly the same as the last. This repeated seven more times until he came to a valve that was partially shut. He could get his hands into the opening but no more.

"Damn. No controls on the inside." he said quietly to himself. "Now what do I do? I can back-track to the first tank and hope that the captain is still there and will respond to a light tapping on the hatch but even if I do, and he does, we'll have to open the valve on the outside and then I'll have to crawl all of the way back in here."

He suddenly thought about the decision to go in after her. Maybe they should have just opened fire on the entire facility, razed it to the ground. No, that would not have worked. The captain could care less if she were to be taken alive or dead but they at least needed a body.

He scanned the area around him, looked for anything that could be stuck into the valve and used to help him pry it open.

"A pipe." he thought, "I need a blasted pipe."

There was none available of course, and he'd not remembered seeing any loose debris in the previous chambers either. The idea he finally settled on was not one that he was very fond of. His proton pistol was long enough and built sturdily enough to function as a lever...but if he broke it that meant facing a well-armed enemy with only his kasik-blade.

"Here goes nothing." he thought, as he jammed the pistol into the opening and pried with all of his might. "Great, it didn't budge."

He tried once again, straining as hard as he could but being cautious not to emit any kind of grunt or sigh that would carry through the hole and into the other chambers. Finally a small squeak of metal against metal, it budged but only just. He rested for a moment before giving it another hard push. This time the valve moved a little more, enough for him to crawl inside and push with his feet. A moment later and he was able to make his way through. Coming

THE YESTERDAY DILEMMA

into the next chamber he lifted his weapon into the light shining through one of the pinholes in the tank's metal. Broken. The coils along the side of the barrel had bent and begun to unravel. It was now junk.

"Huh?!" he gasped as he heard a faint sound reach his ears. Ansul bent to place the useless pistol carefully on the floor and smiled delightfully as he reached for his cherished blade. Its metal zinged slightly as he pulled it free from its scabbard.

"Allright Essa, I'm coming for you." he whispered to himself as he forced his body through the narrow passage. Another empty chamber, but he'd known that. Even through the hand-sized opening he'd initially been presented with he had been able to see most of the current chamber from the other side. He paused, noticed that he also did not *smell* her. Funny, but when a species lives underground like the Martians do, one becomes accustomed to the way smells waft through confined spaces. Two more chambers, nothing. Then with the next he felt certain that he detected just the slightest hint of whatever perfume she'd been foolish enough to have be wearing.

Feeling certain that he was drawing nearer to his prey he decided to stop for just a moment. He removed his boots before proceeding barefoot. The rusted metal, especially with its soft spots, was not something he wished to cut his tender feet on but being without any kind of energy weapon he dared not risk alerting her to his presence before he could get in close. One more chamber, still no one there. The scent had grown stronger though and he swore that he could hear the muffled sound of breathing. A moment later his suspicion was confirmed. Echoing loudly through the maze of tanks and tubes came the chirp of a tele-wave as it came to life. He thought he heard a voice over it briefly, a few words only, before it was silenced. "In system, rendezvous in..." that was all that he could discern from the brief sound. She was in the next chamber, that was certain, and now on ultra-high alert after having given away her location.

With the utmost caution Ansul peered through the valve to see if he could catch sight of her. He did. She was standing near the middle of the chamber, back pressed against a support beam, breathing heavily and with her weapon drawn. He would have to wait.

Sitting just out of her view, had she looked behind her through the valve, he rested against one of the metal walls of the tank. He waited there for some fifteen minutes or more. He thought about how the wall he rested on felt weak, how in a few more years rust would overtake it and leave a gaping hole in the tank. Suddenly there was shuffling of feet. Essa Von Braun was moving. It was a gamble, but he needed to take a look. She shouldn't be able to see very well at all in such a dark place, but even the remotest chance of being spotted and shot with that awful weapon of hers was unnerving. As briefly as possible Ansul poked his head into the opening. She was going the other way.

He jumped into action, slipping through the valve that connected the two chambers. He was unable to remain as quiet as he'd hoped. As he'd entered the tank the fabric of his pants caught on a rusted piece of metal and made the faintest tearing sound. He froze, watched as she turned around and pointed her gun in his direction.

"Can she see me?" he asked himself in terror.

Her eyes darted slightly left, then slightly right. No, she could not see him. He half expected her to simply open fire in his general direction but he knew her to be a clever woman, knew that she'd not give away her position to those on the outside so casually. Carefully and deliberately Ansul moved a few paces to the right, closer to the tank wall, feeling for any weak spots in the floor.

"I know you're in here!" she called out, the sound echoed loudly inside the tank. The Martian had not expected her to do so.

He cupped his left hand over his mouth in a fashion that left the right side of it uncovered so as to direct the sound of his voice in that direction. "You are mine Essa Von Braun." he said in a low and ghostly tone.

In the dim light he could see her clearly, watched as she spun around to face the opposite direction. Now! He rushed her from behind but she was quicker than he'd anticipated. She spun to point the deadly KA7Z at him but he was already too close. A quick slash at her wrist from the kasik-blade caused it to clatter to the floor. Ansul ducked a wild left swing but failed to dodge her boot as it came up and planted itself into his sternum. He fell back onto the floor, winded.

"It's been nearly a damned hour." Tarsik fumed under his breath. "Where the hell are you Ansul?"

Just then he was startled by the sudden collapse of the side of one of the water tanks not more than 10 meters from where he was standing. It crumbled to the ground, kicking a massive plume of dust up into the air.

Ansul knew he'd had her on the ropes but she'd tackled him hard into the side of the tank wall as a last resort and they'd both come crashing through. As they hit the ground he dropped his kasik-blade in an instinctual attempt to shield his eyes, which burned like fire in an instant, from the fierce light of the white dwarf. Essa lay still, on top of him, for perhaps two or three seconds, then apparently came to her senses. He felt her thrash about, going for the blade which he'd dropped. Ansul pulled his hands away from his eyes, determining to instead shut them tightly since his goggles were nowhere to be found on his head. He grappled with her as she reached for the razor sharp knife. Their hands grasped onto it simultaneously, it felt slippery, covered in the loose planetary dust. She managed to pry it loose from his grasp and Ansul could only open his eyes for an instant to see her bringing it above her head. He knew what was to follow and crossed his arms over his chest to block the deadly blow.

A quick energetic cracking sound and her thighs, which had grasped him so tightly, went lip. She collapsed down onto him. He felt the pain of the blade as it dug into the flesh of his left forearm but it had not been a blow with power behind it. Instead it was merely the result of her fall as the proton bolt from the PRK8 marksrifle that Jones' had commandeered from the fallen Zulian tore through her spine, rendering her dead before she knew she'd even been hit.

20\\

The ejection module, no more than the cockpit and a small life-support system, of the F-Type hovered over the loading bay's deck without a sound. No sound in a vacuum. Tarsik stood on the upper level of the loading bay holding a grav-ray, a device that uses an artificial gravity beam to guide large objects in space. He'd meant for some time to get one of the nice automated overhead units installed but had yet to get around to it. He stared out through the polymer of his helmet, its surface only ever-so slightly splitting the light of the capsule's emergency flashers into a spectrum.

The magnetic plates of his boots firmly attached to the metal floor, for the bay's gravity had been turned down to zero, it took Tarsik slow but steady effort to reel the capsule in. Once it was inside he set it down onto the deck as gently as possible. If its occupant was indeed who he *hoped* it was he didn't wish to irritate her any further. He already knew she'd have quite the temper.

After releasing the grav-ray he placed the bulky double-handled device into a nearby gear cage before flipping the switch that would close the door, restore the gravity and re-pressurize the bay.

"Did I just abduct a passerby?" he thought to himself, keenly aware of the hiss of air rushing back into the space around him. Scanners had indicated that the occupant was *likely* human but they could discern little else. He was taking a huge chance, possibly adding kidnapping to the *Honshu* crews' list of offenses.

The light over the door behind him switched from red to green with an audible click and a few seconds later it slid open, allowing Pilot Jones and Doctor Ramus into the bay. Tarsik turned toward them, facing them with his good eye.

"You know she's going to be pissed right?" Jones asked. The captain barely caught what she said as he was in the process of removing his bubble-helmet.

"*If* it is who we think it is I have no doubt about that Pilot."

"I'd better check her to ensure that she's okay." the doctor commented before grabbing on to the cold metal railing and taking a step down the ramp.

He was greeted with sharp words from the captain. "Hold it Doctor." to which Ramus turned to see his commander standing there holding up a hand, "You think for a second she's not waiting in there with a blaster?"

"A valid concern." the doctor smiled. "Then how shall we proceed?"

"I've got it." Jones remarked, lifting the device she'd been holding at her side to belly level and tapping a few keys on it. "If it worked to get her on-board it'll work to get that thing open as well."

Her fingers moved quickly, tapping at heavily sprung keys on the rectangular box that responded to her touch with metallic clicking noises. The orange status light near the top briefly dimmed, lit up green, then faded and went back to orange. The lights were accompanied by a sound that could only be described as mechanical annoyance. The sharp noise echoed in the mostly empty loading bay and Jones smacked the device on its side with the palm of her left hand.

"C'mon you piece of space trash." the remote console was nearly as old as the *Honshu*'s keel herself, but it was functioning properly.

"It's not the console." Tarsik blurted, "She's engaged the manual overrides. We caught her by surprise out in space but now she's hunkered down...great." while the circumstances were frustrating he found himself almost completely certain that they were dealing with Emily Faust.

"So what now? I seriously doubt that blasting her out of there is going to do anything for her disposition Captain." the doctor said flatly.

Tarsik didn't respond, rather he tapped at his tele-wave, setting it to a wide frequency range, then spoke. "Emily if that's you in there I need you to come on out okay? It's Captain Tarsik."

The three stood there for a moment in silence. The door behind them, still open, allowed in the sounds of several crewmen coming down the hallway. They were carrying sidearms, to provide backup in case it should be needed. As they rounded the corner Tarsik lifted his hand to have them hold there.

"Look," he spoke into his tele-wave again, "I know none of this makes sense. I got notified of a contract I never accepted and then when I investigated it I get police cruisers sent out to arrest me. I promise you I'm every bit as confused as you are but I need your help to make sense of it."

The cracking of a seal and the resulting hiss of air, though minuscule compared with the volume of the room, was still easily heard in the echoing space. The captain watched as a crack, one just large enough for the barrel of a weapon, appeared along the seam where the capsule's cockpit glass met the metal of the fuselage. Just as he'd predicted the tip of a pistol did indeed protrude from it, accompanied by a voice yelling through the crack. "*You're not Captain Tarsik, who in the hell are you?*"

"Emily," he spoke loudly, ignoring the tele-wave and instead going for the more personal approach, "I swear to you that I am who I say I am. I was actually hoping you could tell me who in the space-blasted hell is out there running around claiming to *be* me."

"Nice try." came the response, "And for the life of me I can't figure out what you think you'll gain by this but Captain Tarsik doesn't have an eye patch, the doctor has *never* had a mustache and I sure as hell would never be caught dead wearing my hair like that."

Pilot Jones' eyes grew wide. What in the stars was wrong with her hair? Long bangs, short back spiked in every direction, tips colored a vibrant purple-blue...it was all the rage in two galaxies! "What the hell is that supposed to mean?" she wanted to yell out, but knew that it wasn't the appropriate time.

"Pilot," Doctor Ramus tried his luck, "you're absolutely right. There would be no benefit in us deceiving you. We're your friends...at least *versions* of your friends...and we are simply looking for your help."

"And you couldn't just wave me?" she shouted through the cockpit seal, "Maybe talking would have been better than hijacking my ship's controls and forcing me to eject before hauling me aboard your counterfeit green *Honshu*."

"Doctor..." Tarsik said but Yatin ignored his protest and continued down the ramp toward the capsule. He came to a stop about two meters in front of the barrel protruding from the seal and held his hands up.

"I'm not armed Pilot. Please put down the gun and come out and talk to us."

He listened, more nervously than he'd have admitted to, waiting for a response. There was a short silence, then the barrel retracted into the cockpit and the glass lifted slightly. Inside he could see the confused face of Emily Faust, her lovely blonde hair pulled back into a messy ponytail just like he remembered from when she'd first come aboard the ship, long before she'd met and married the knave Horatio Jones. The doctor beamed and she seemed to respond to the smile. He had no way of knowing the guilt that she associated with him, the reminder of her own failure.

"That's it." he said softly as she lifted the cockpit glass and began to climb from the capsule. He put out a hand to help her down.

"Doctor..." Tarsik warned loudly from his spot at the top of the ramp that led from the floor of the loading bay to its upper level and the door which led to the rest of the ship.

As her boot touched metal she gripped Ramus' hand tightly and spun it around behind his back before pulling the pistol from where it had been, tucked into her belt at the small of her back. She placed it against his right temple.

"Proton pistol at point-blank range Captain!" she yelled up at the obviously fake Tarsik, "What do I find when I blow his head off, huh? A bunch of circuits and wires? Are you all a bunch of Autoks or something?"

Tarsik shook his head, holding his hand clear of his sidearm and making sure to let the fear show in his face. "We're not clones, we're not Autoks. Damn it Faust we're you're friends!" he said using her maiden name. "You shoot the doctor in the head and his blood's going to be on your hands...literally."

"Pilot I can assure you that I am *not* a threat." Ramus said lowly, through clenched teeth.

"Why did you attack my ship?" Faust demanded of the captain.

"We were running from police cruisers Emily. We didn't have time to play twenty questions with you. Jones here exploited a known weakness in the security protocols of the old F-Type and ejected your capsule so that we could bring you aboard. I'm sorry for that." as Tarsik spoke he began to walk slowly and as non-threateningly as possible down the ramp.

"Jones?" she asked, her eyes scanning the upper level.

"Yoohoo." Pilot Jones waved at her. "I got married ya numbskull."

Faust was taken aback, "Not...please tell me it's not Horatio Jones?!"

"What? How the hell do you...?"

Jones was cut off by a motion from her commander.

"That doesn't matter right now Emily. Point the gun at me." Tarsik pointed to his own chest. "Go ahead. Point it at me and let the doctor go okay?"

He watched as she glanced at Jones on the upper level, no doubt making sure that she wasn't going for a weapon, then quickly switched her aim from Ramus' head to the captain's sternum. With a quick shove she pushed the doctor away from her. He didn't hesitate, taking the opportunity to quickly scramble up the ramp to join Jones.

"I need an explanation!" she snapped.

"I *really* wish I could give you one but like I said before I was actually hoping that you could help *us* out in that department."

"Where did you *come* from?" she asked angrily.

"We were just going about our business, wrapping up a contract on Dathon VII, when we got forwarded a copy of a contract that we'd never accepted. We tried investigating but something is very wrong. First the Casidaen authorities think we're imposters, now you! You'll understand if that doesn't make a whole hell of a lot of sense to me since as far as I know my ship has *always* been green, the doctor has *always* had a mustache, I lost the eye six years ago, and I've lived my entire life up to this point without my being Captain Harridor Tarsik of the R.S. *Honshu* having ever being questioned before."

A notion, a seemingly impossible one, popped into Faust's head, "Uh oh."

"Uh oh what?" Tarsik asked cautiously.

"I think I just *might* know what's going on."

"And that would be...?" Tarsik was motioning for her

to lower the gun that was aimed at his chest.

"The *Honshu*, well *my Honshu*, recently had a little accident and ended up in the distant past. Maybe we changed something? It never occurred to me that we might be the ones out of place if we altered the timeline."

"Time travel is impossible Emily." the captain stated, his gaze still locked on the weapon. "Please put the gun down. You're making me more than a tad nervous."

She eyed him for a minute and then reluctantly agreed. She holstered it but kept her hand on it.

"Yeah here's the thing, Ansul also swore up and down the space-lanes that time travel was impossible but we sure as hell did it. Ended up on Earth and got to meet a few dinosaurs face to face."

A slight chuckle came from Pilot Jones. Faust glared at her. It unnerved Jones, she knew what that stare meant and somehow that gave it more gravity.

"So let's just say that you really *did* travel to the past." the doctor began, "How would that account for two crews and two *Honshus*?"

"Hell if I know." Faust shrugged.

The doctor rubbed his chin. He was a student of many disciplines but knew very little about theoretical physics. Still the subject intrigued him. "Perhaps if you somehow changed the past then when you reemerged into the present you brought those changes along with you into this reality."

"No." Tarsik chimed in, "If that were the case then why are *we* being treated like the strangers? Wouldn't *they* be the strangers here?"

"Let me ask you this," the doctor mused, "have you noticed anything different since returning to the present?"

"Besides an alternative version of the *Honshu* and her crew?" Emily smirked, "No. You're the only thing different." she pointed to Tarsik, "Your service uniform is the wrong color but it was the correct one for every Serviceman I saw on Tersis."

The three stood there in deep thought for a moment.

"It would appear that *we* are the ones in an alternate reality." Doctor Ramus said to himself, then to the others, "That makes little sense. It should be the other way around."

"Wait, where did you emerge back into the present?" Jones asked her doppelganger.

"Inside the Crux." she replied, "We were in a firefight and had to engage NC inside the anomaly, that's what caused the time travel incident in the first place."

"My counterpart ordered that? He must be fool!" Tarsik said, trying to mask his contempt for this man who had stolen his identity.

"It was that or get deep-fried by a vulcan cannon." Faust quipped.

"Ah." the captain sighed, "Well then, guess I can't blame him too much. That's no way to go out."

Jones waved her hands, as if to silence the unproductive chatter, "Okay we didn't start off inside the Crux. That blows *my* theory."

"Which was?" the doctor asked.

"That when they blasted back into the present they somehow dragged us along for the ride from another dimension, caused us to pop into this universe...but we were dozens of parsecs away from the Crux. You'd think we'd have emerged from the same point in space."

"Besides," Tarsik stated, "wouldn't we *remember* popping into another reality? Something would have shifted right? We'd have noticed some immediate difference surely."

"Well we were sitting on a featureless salt-pan at the time. I suppose not much would have changed there." Yatin chimed in.

"Just an idea here." Faust spoke up, "We could contact Aeolus Station, see if they've noticed anything strange from the area of space where we emerged."

All four looked around at each other, none seemed to

have a better idea.

"Seems like a simple enough thing." Tarsik commented. "You'll understand if we ask you to disarm before following us to the cockpit though, won't you Emily?"

"Look I'll help you try to figure out this situation but I'm taking my capsule and getting back to my ship."

"We can't do that at the moment I'm afraid." Tarsik said.

"And why not?" she eyed him suspiciously.

"Well, we were being chased by police cruisers as I mentioned. As soon as we got you aboard we activated NC and jumped clear of the patrol."

"And left my ship there to be confiscated?!" she cried out and slapped the strange version of her old captain squarely across the jaw.

He rubbed it for a moment before looking at her, anger flashing in his eyes. "We used to carry a small craft ourselves a few years back so we have moorings for one. She's anchored to the outside of the *Honshu* and we're going to send some maintenance bots out to make sure she hasn't sustained any damage before we send you back to her. Now...let's head to the cockpit and place that call shall we?"

He motioned toward the ramp. Faust handed him her pistol as she walked past him.

He spoke to her back, "I'm not sure how *your* Captain Tarsik did things but if you slap me like that again I'll break a few teeth out of your skull." he said to her back.

"Yep," she replied without turning back, "that sounds like my captain. Still...you deserved it." she chuckled.

Suddenly the bay's intercom crackled to life. It was Herschel. "Captain the cruisers are on us again!"

Tarsik let out an angry growl and pushed past the others on his way to the lift.

"Bastards are persistent, I'll give them that."

21\\

Most of the crew had already departed the *Honshu* hours ago but Tarsik, Ansul, and a few others had stayed behind to get in a little face time with the refit crew of the Lorandis orbital docks to ensure that they were aware of the extensive modifications that the ship had undergone over the years. Tarsik had formally dismissed the vast majority of the auxiliary crew. The *Honshu* was likely to be in dry-dock for up to three months and he understood that the men needed open contracts in order to sign on to other Service ships that might be passing through.

Much to his surprise both Jones and Fizril had requested to stay on, despite the excessive layover. The big cat didn't catch him off guard as much, as he seemed to be loyal almost to a fault. Jones, however, he'd have taken for a man who'd jump ship and move on to greener pastures if the credit flow dried up. He'd been wrong before though. After all, Ansul had joined the *Honshu* crew as an auxiliary but before the end of his first hitch had proven himself to be a far more competent mechanic than the aging and hard to deal with Jorel McQueary who had been the ship's engineer since her relaunch as *Honshu* six months prior.

He could definitely see how Fizril's powerful

physique and lightning fast reflexes would serve them well and there was a part of him that hoped to eventually add the Antarian to the regular crew. Jones on the other hand, while deadly with a proton blaster, would need to get his drinking problem under control if he ever had any hopes of remaining onboard long-term. The captain would tolerate a bit of a penchant for drinking from his men, in fact it was even expected to some degree, but not while on an active mission and he retained the rights to break contract with any man who let it interfere with his duties.

"Orbital shuttle one-three-one now arriving." the station's synthesized AI voice called out over the loudspeaker.

"That us?." Ansul questioned, sitting atop the pile of luggage that carried most of the worldly goods that he, Captain Tarsik, and crewmen Fizril and Jones possessed.

They had been expecting another one of the facility's docking pods and not an orbital shuttle.

Fizril was reclining against the rear wall, flicking his tail about in agitation. Jones stared out of the small glass panes that surrounded the circular airlock, taking a small sip of the contents of his pocket flask.

"Yep." Jones chimed in, "Definitely a shuttle, looks like a security one in fact."

"Uh oh," Ansul smiled, "What'd you do?" he then laughed aloud at his own remark.

"Hmmph." was all that the crewman responded. Tarsik's hand instinctively went to the tele-wave at his belt but he held back. Whoever they were he'd be speaking with them face to face in less than a minute anyway. The captain took a moment to walk over to where Fizril was leaning against the transparent titanium wall. He looked out at his ship which was anchored in place by several large docking arms and illuminated from all directions by bright flood lights. It hung there on its side in the middle of the massive dry-dock. A handful of the facility's inspectors were already milling about inspecting the heavily damaged rear fins and proton cannons.

The dock master had assured him that the *Honshu* was in good hands, especially with IPH footing the bill for top-notch parts. Still Tarsik wavered. He much preferred leaving the old girl in the care of Ansul or even the Novan engineers who'd performed much of her upgrades over the years. He touched his hand to the floor-to-ceiling window and gave her one last look.

"You know...that's really sweet Captain." Ansul quipped. "I'm sure she'll miss you too."

"My foot!" Tarsik turned and snapped, "You and I will both be up here at least twice a week to make sure these atoms-for-brains aren't screwing up the old girl."

Ansul smiled and nodded, lightly rocking atop the pile of luggage that he was perched on, "No complaints from me. Just the thought of them goofing up the countless hours of fine tuning I've done to the power grid and reactor systems is enough to make my skin crawl. If you don't mind Harry I'm going to be up here every chance I get."

"You don't want to take a nice vacation on a prime world?" Jones asked sincerely. "I know I sure will be taking advantage of everything Tersis has to offer."

"Oh I don't doubt it." the Martian retorted snidely, making a gesture like he was drinking a bottle of whiskey.

Jones waved him off, "Ansul it's just a ship. These fellas have it well under control. You're really denying yourself an experience if you don't get out and explore the planet a bit."

"Hah!" Fizril laughed aloud, startling them all. Then, in a bellowing tone, "Just a ship?" he wagged his finger at Jones, "So you see the *Honshu* only as a means of getting from one place to another?"

Jones shrugged, "Well...kinda...yeah."

"A true spacer..." Fizril stepped forward, "treats his vessel as he would a member of his family."

"Oh yeah, I read something about that." Tarsik chimed

in, "aren't Antarian rockets typically kept in a family for generations?"

The big cat turned and gave the human a toothy grin, "Yes. A hull can be passed down for many generations, with each generation of spacer performing upgrades to keep the ship relevant to the era in which it serves."

"Sound familiar?" Ansul asked the captain.

"Indeed." he smiled, "No need to replace something that's still perfectly good, just make alterations as needed."

Fizril only grinned and gave a slight bow of his head.

The sound of the orbital shuttle's docking clamps making contact with the airlock's own drew all of their attention. Ansul stood and grabbed his bags, tossing them over his shoulder. "So you uh...you spend a lot of time on prime worlds there Mr. Jones?" he asked.

Jones tried to mask his almost involuntary reaction to the question. "No...no..." he stammered, "but you know...I've set boot on a few of them." he then smiled at the Martian, "A lot more to do than just drink and gamble Ansul, unlike those backwater floats and dirtballs that we so often find ourselves at."

"Ah," Tarsik finally chimed in, "So you only drink like you do because there aren't other activities to be had?"

The crewman had his reasons for drinking and he damned well didn't feel obliged to get all touchy feely and start sharing his feelings so he decided instead to brush the question aside.

"Look," he said as he lifted his overladen bag from the deck with the aid of its shoulder strap, "all that I'm saying is that a world like Tersis has got a whole lot of things to keep you busy...things like beaches, hiking trails, art museums, theatre, hunting..."

"Hunting?" Fizril's ears perked up.

"You betcha big guy." Jones clicked his tongue and pointed a finger-gun at the Antarian.

Ansul let his head bobble about as he went over the possibilities. "I guess I get your point Crewman," he said, "but tell me one thing?"

"Sure." Jones shot back.

"You really into the theatre?"

Jones was about to fire off a witty retort when the airlock door mechanisms began to whir furiously. The large circular door vented a bit of atmosphere and then slid into the wall. There was a tall and very sturdily built figure standing in the airlock. A female one, Tarsik thought. The heavy gear the figure wore made that unclear however, as did the closely cropped reddish-blonde hair. He lifted his hand to silence his men.

As the steam from the ice crystals in the airlock dispersed the tall figure took a few steps forward, out into the corridor to greet the spacers.

"Lieutenant Commander Shirley Mitchell, Casidaen Security Forces." she spoke.

"I assume there's a reason that you were sent to pick us up instead of the taxi jocks who ferried the rest of my men down to Tersis."

"Aye sir." she said respectively, not making direct eye contact like a good little soldier. "At seventeen-hundred hours system police forces intercepted and detained this vessel...:" she detached a small portable viewer from her belt and brought it up to the captain's face.

"Looks like an IPC Type -7 like the *Honshu*. What of it?"

The commander pushed a button on the viewer and the image changed from that of the green rocket that it had been displaying to one of a much more curious nature.

"I don't get it. Is this a joke?" Tarsik asked the woman.

"Negative Sir. This man claims to be Captain Harridor Tarsik of the R.S. *Honshu*. He apparently has access to your personal Service security cipher."

Tarsik just stood frozen for a moment, his brow wrinkled in thought, before he looked up at the woman and let out a confused, "What?!"

"The situation is even more complex Captain. They

sent me to retrieve you and to take you to security headquarters immediately. I will brief you once we're underway."

Tarsik thought for a moment and then nodded his agreement. "You heard the lady. Grab your shit and get it stowed."

Their belongings were quickly loaded with the help of the security officer and they departed the Lorandis docks with haste. A few minutes later, aboard orbital shuttle 131, Lt. Commander Mitchell spun around in her copilot's seat to face the Servicemen.

"I'll be brief. We've got a rapidly developing situation here. The duplicate *Honshu* was taken into custody an hour ago and our men performed detailed scans both of it and of its crew. There was found to be an anomaly in their quantum rhythmic signatures."

"Meaning...?" Jones asked from the back.

Ansul sat forward in his seat, his mouth agape. "Meaning they're not from this dimension!"

"Seriously?" Jones asked, "You believe in alternate dimensions but not in time travel?"

Ansul turned to the crewman, "Well obviously my views have changed somewhat over the last few days when it comes to time travel now haven't they? And yes," he continued, "quantum-level vibration signature mismatches in matter can literally mean only one thing; that an object or person, is somehow extra-dimensional."

"Gentlemen." Mitchell interrupted the two who promptly ceased their chatter and returned their attention to her. "Mr. Ansul is correct. Everything in our universe vibrates with a certain quantum signature. Anything displaying a variation on this signature can *only* be extra-dimensional."

Ansul gave Jones an "I told you so" grin before turning back to the commander and giving her a sarcastic "You may continue." gesture.

The lieutenant commander was not used to interacting

with Servicemen. She found their lack of strict discipline extremely frustrating but carried on with her briefing.

"What's more we received this from Aeolus Station less than one half hour ago."

Her long gracile fingers tapped away at a few of the gem-like keys on the shuttle's control panel and a screen folded down from above. It crackled to life and on it was a face that Tarsik immediately recognized. It was Deutron Cal, captain of the *Prometheus*. He seemed disheveled and the bags under his eyes signified that he'd not slept in some time.

"To anyone who this signal reaches this is Deutron Cal, acting commander of the Interplanetary Holdings space station *Aeolus*. I am sending out this message to warn all space traffic to avoid the Crux and its surrounding vicinity. There is something happening here aboard the station that we cannot explain and its effects seem to be accelerating. Entire sections of the station are experiencing system failures and even those sections with which we are still in contact are showing signs of some form of temporal or dimensional distortions that are resulting in..."

The image flickered as the signal appeared to waver in strength. When it came back Deutron Cal's uniform and the uniform of those around him had changed. He also now sported a well-manicured mustache in place of the short trimmed goatee he was wearing only seconds before.

"I..." he began to mutter than trailed off, "This is Deutron Cal, station commander of Aeolus Station. I...I can't seem to remember why I was sending this message. My apologies. Please disregard it in its entirety."

The image disappeared from the screen and was replaced by the CSSF logo momentarily before it folded itself neatly back into the ceiling where it had come from.

"That's..." Ansul said, his mouth hanging open and his eyes wide, "that's um..."

"The astrophysicists we consulted at the Tersian Science Academy are calling it 'trans-dimensional displacement' but what that actually means is above my pay grade." Mitchell finished.

Ansul turned to his captain, grabbing him by the shoulder, "When we engaged NC inside the Crux we must have created some kind of dimensional bleed."

"Yeah, that or the captain here shooting a dinosaur in the face caused some kind of butterfly effect that's changing time." Jones posited.

"No, I don't think so." Ansul said, being uncharacteristically serious. "Look, there's a thousand reasons that I never believed time travel to be possible...and honestly it still *shouldn't* be...but what if it's actually a combination of the two?"

Tarsik, Fizril, Jones and Commander Mitchell all waited for him to continue.

Ansul got up onto his knees in his seat, his mind whirling with so many possibilities he didn't feel like he had the capacity to stay strapped in.

"Okay...it's like you said Jones. Harry shot Mr. T-Rex dead right after we crashed." he made a gun with his right hand and mimicked firing off a shot, "but then we also interacted with other plants and animals while we were on Earth...Earth 65 million BC or so. It's possible that we created an entirely new timeline that never existed before we did those things and that somehow we..." he searched for the word, "we *dragged* that reality into this one when we came back."

"So what you're saying is?" Tarsik grumbled.

"That what's going on is literally both things; a combination of a temporal ripple effect coupled with a dimensional crossover." he fumbled in the pocket of his mechanic's jacket briefly before producing a grease pen that he used when cutting metal.

"No you can't..." Mitchell attempted protest as the Martian began to draw on the wall of the shuttle.

He crudely drew two circles, one with the letter A drawn inside of it and one with the letter B.

"Now imagine these two distinct realities, one we may or may not have created by affecting past events..."

"Uh huh." Tarsik moaned as he encouraged Ansul to get to the point.

"Imagine a hand reaching out from each one of them, grasping onto the rim of each dimensional portal," he quickly and rather poorly drew the hands he was speaking of, "and then each one trying to pull the other dimension into its own."

It was clear from their blank expressions that no one was following so he grunted in frustration before returning to the wall to draw what looked like a partially folded circle.

"A Mobius strip, you're familiar with the concept right?"

Everyone present nodded.

"It's kind of like that, with each dimension being one side of the strip...but the strip is continuous so they're separate but also not really separate."

"My brain hurts." Jones piped up, then took another sip from his flask.

Ansul attempted to erase the scribbles on the wall of the shuttle with his sleeve but had little luck and abandoned the effort entirely.

"Sorry about that." he said to the lieutenant commander, "I'm sure maintenance can..."

She cut him off, "Yes, I'm sure they'll figure it out. Can you please finish what you were trying to say?"

"I think the two timelines are trying to merge...or maybe flip-flop and that somehow what's happening on Aeolus is part of how there's now a second *Honshu*." he sighed, "And what worries me is that I'm not sure it's going to just stop. If the two realities flip I think we might find ourselves in the other one...the one where IPH uniforms have vertical stripes like we saw Deutron Cal's change to and where the *Honshu* is green instead of blue and yep...where Captain Tarsik has a fraggin eye patch!"

"But Deutron Cal changed in front of our eyes, there wasn't a duplicate of him. How are there duplicates of the *Honshu* and its crew?"

"Maybe..." Jones chimed in, "it's because *we* were the ones who did the whole ripping the dimensions a new one thing, ya know?"

Ansul pointed to him, "Yeah, that's my best guess too."

"Are you sure about any of this Ansul?"

The Martian looked flustered, "What?! No! I'm a space-blasted mechanic, not an expert on temporal mechanics. I'm literally just tossing out theories. How did you guys not get that? My crude drawings and bumbling pseudo-explanations didn't get that across?"

Tarsik rubbed his temples in an attempt to stymie a migraine that was steadily growing in intensity. Just then his tele-wave beeped.

"What now?" he thought to himself, "And from who?"

He tapped the button, "Go for Tarsik."

"Captain," Doctor Ramus' voice had a clear tone of concern to it, "I'm afraid we have a problem."

Jones slouched in his seat and took another swig from his flask. "What else is new? "

22\\

The tattered fabric of Tamin Thezal's robes made harsh flapping sounds in the wind that were only barely audible to him over the overlapping sounds of the ceremonial shofar horns sounding out their calls across the plain. The briny sands of Dathon tore at his visor as he pushed his way through abandoned alleyways. So thick was the dust cloud that the light of Hatal, the planet's primary star, could only throw a diffuse sienna glow over the village. Blood pulsed through the young man's veins, the feeling of it was electrifying. The fruition of the life work of so many men had led to this moment. Most of them had long since joined the dust of Dathon but Tamin felt very alive in this moment; a true witness to history. The glowing embers that blew about the deserted streets seemed to his mind a cleansing fire.

The men outside the sheikh's tent were almost certainly ones that Tamin knew quite well but they were bundled beneath layers even thicker than his own so he could not identify them. Regardless they stood aside and parted the flaps of the old style tent in a hurried fashion that matched the young mullah's pace. Sheikh Mamad Al'taman still insisted upon living in a tent, to honor the old ways, but

THE YESTERDAY DILEMMA

Tamin knew him to be a forward-thinking visionary. He appreciated the sheikh's reverence for the past, but more than anything it was his unmitigated gall and his contempt for those who would rest upon their laurels for all time while the people of Dathon suffered needlessly that made him the man Tamin respected most in the world. The cunning old man was not like the other sheikhs. Al'taman grabbed fate like one would grab a bull by the horns and he pointed it to water where others would have let it dry into a husk. The sheikh was a man of destiny, just as Tamin felt himself to be.

Only the smallest slit of light entered the cavernous black space of the sheikh's tent but Tamin knew precisely where his master sat. From the darkness deceptively frail fingers reached out to him and motioned for him to come closer. The third mullah removed his goggles and head wraps and placed them on the dirt floor to his side before taking three steps forward and dropping down onto one knee, his head bowed in a show of respect.

"Raise your head my son." came the gravelly old voice, almost inaudible over the roar of the rockets and the howl of the dust-laden winds they stirred beating at the canvas of the tent.

Tamin did as was commanded of him. Adjusting to the dark his eyes began to make out the familiar face of the sheikh. Gaunt and with a heavy beard of grey and white it wore a smile.

"You are pleased my sheikh?" he asked sincerely

The old man lifted his hands to about the height of his face and shook them joyously. "My ears hear the sound," he said, "the sound of change upon the wind."

He was clearly referencing the sound of the rockets outside the village lifting the tons and tons of elorite that they'd accumulated over the years into orbit. He looked directly at Tamin with such stillness in him. The mullah was sure that the old man's eyes could not see him, for they had long ago glazed over

"The sound..." he went on, "...is a joyous one." at that he smiled broadly, "Better still my eyes can see...they can see the coming of the light of Deliah. And that light...oh my boy that light will remake this world for all time."

He reached up and placed his bony hand against the younger man's cheek.

"It will be the last thing that I ever see." his words cut the darkness between them. Tamin had known for some time that the old sheikh was not long for this world. "But *your* eyes..." the sheikh said smiling, "they are the same as mine."

He withdrew his hand shakily and touched his own face. Tamin knew what Al'taman meant. He had never been able before to say it aloud but both of them knew that Tamin was of the old man's blood.

"Your eyes..." he said reverently, staring off into the darkness of the tent, "they will see the glory of our new home."

Tamin choked back a tear. He wished so desperately that destiny had afforded he and his elderly father a more normal relationship, but remaking an entire world required strategy and sacrifice.

"Yes...Sheikh."

The elder's blurry gaze returned to the face of his son. A pained expression crossed over his face ever so briefly and then a single tear rolled down the old man's cheek.

"Only now..." he said in his gravelly tone, "sitting in the shadow of the worldshaper with Deliah's heralds ascending to her thrown am I able to speak plain truth to you my son. I have loved you, and your brothers and sisters, and all of those on Dathon so much that I have done unspeakable things to bring about this day."

Tamin's thoughts turned to his own unspeakable acts, those committed only minutes before in the courtyard, and as if reading the mind of his son Al'taman spoke, "So it is done?"

"Yes Sheikh." the mullah responded wearily.

"Remember always," the old man said slowly and deliberately, "that our people will need a leader who looks to the future. Not one that dwells in the past."

"I understand." Tamin nodded. "May Yadra forgive me."

"May Yadra forgive us *all* my son."

"You believe it, do you not?"

"I do," the old sheikh nodded, "I must."

Tamin only nodded but somehow he knew that his blind old father understood the gesture.

The roar of the rockets outside seemed to rise to a crescendo before slowly starting to level off and then fade away. Tamin allowed himself for the first time in his life to touch the sheikh's hand. He felt frailty in the embrace. Al'taman's time on Dathon was truly drawing to an end. Tamin believed it to be only through sheer force of will that the man had hung on for one-hundred and eleven years.

Outside the shofars fell silent. Tamin felt his father's feeble hand stiffen in his own. A moment later the shofars sounded again, but this time they sounded the call to battle.

"To the last very moment," the old sheikh smiled and shook his head, "they shall fight their own salvation."

The distant sound of skimmer engines being pushed beyond their limits pricked up Tamin's ears. The old man seemed to hear them too.

"They are too late to stop the reformation, Deliah's heralds have ascended!" the younger man attempted to reassure himself as well as his father.

"Go my son." Al'taman urged, "The column of smoke and dust from the heralds will have appeared as no less than the greatest of sandstorms to every eye on the horizon. They cannot stop Deliah's prophecy, but they *can* slaughter our people for our perceived arrogance.", he clasped the younger man's hand tightly, "Save everyone that you can."

Tamin, without thinking, kissed the old man on the cheek before hurrying to his feet. He grabbed his goggles and wraps and made for the door. He stopped just shy of it and turned to ask one final question.

"Hassad, Hajan, were they my brothers?" he referred to the first and second mullahs whose throats he had slit only moments before in the courtyard, after they had been caught attempting to subvert the sheikh's plans by sabotaging the rockets.

"They were..." the old voice spoke softly from the darkness, "the brothers of Tamin Thezal. But now you have no brothers my son, for you are Tamin Al'taman, sheikh of the village of Qadir, and first emissary of Deliah herself."

23\\

The orbital shuttle's ramp had not even touched the landing pad atop the security complex when Captain Tarsik jumped to the deck, the metal plates in his boots ringing out audibly despite the roar of the engines. He strode toward the doctor with a furious look on his face. Doctor Ramus knew that the captain's emotions were not directed at him but were instead a mere reflection of the frustration the man felt with the current situation.

The doctor covered his eyes momentarily as the shuttle's engines flared, kicking up dust and sending it his way. The captain approached and put his arm around the doctor's shoulders and led him a short distance away from the landing pad.

"Show me." he demanded curtly.

The doctor lifted up a portable screen and tapped at the buttons along the left edge. An image of a body scan appeared. "I was going stir crazy after being released from the hospital and decided to file my report, as ship's physician, with Service Central Authority. Imagine my surprise when I pull up the Service record file of Essa Von Braun only to see that I knew her from the war."

The color drained from Tarsik's face. "You mean....?"

The doctor nodded and tapped at his own head. "She had a Lazarus node, just like me."

The frustration in the captain's voice only seemed to grow, "How is that even possible?"

"Fate, it seems, is indeed a cruel mistress Captain. You see...she was aboard the *Babylonia*..."

Tarsik cut the older man off mid-sentence, "The hulk that we found you on all those years ago?"

"Mmm hmm," the doctor zoomed in the image on his portable screen, "the node's visible here." he said, indicating the foreign body that showed up clearly in the scan. "She's a little older of course but if only I'd seen her before today I would have recognized her immediately."

"Where'd you get this scan?" Tarsik asked with genuine curiosity.

"Tersians..." Ramus muttered, then waved his arm at the city around them, "I'll give them on thing, they're certainly thorough. When I pulled up her file there was a post-mortem body scan attached from the Tersian Security Ministry. The presence of her Lazarus node confirmed what my memory told me and I waved in immediately to alert them to the fact that they needed to send a security detail down to the morgue but I must have been a few minutes too late."

"And that node definitely will *not* work a second time, correct?"

"Are you asking me if she'll stay dead the next time you kill her?" the doctor quipped with a smile.

The captain nodded and returned the gesture, allowing his angry grimace to subside only momentarily, "That's exactly what I'm asking."

Just then the captain's eyes shifted to something behind the doctor. He spun to see Minister Felize coming through the doors that led to the rooftop landing pad accompanied by four armed men.

"How did you know what she would do?" the minister demanded, in a tone that was almost accusatory.

"It's not that complicated," Ansul interjected as he strode up the ramp, "she tends to stick to the greatest hits." he chuckled, "Get in trouble, steal ship, hurt anyone who gets in her way."

"Mr. Ansul you'll have to forgive me if I don't find the situation in any way amusing. I have two men dead and two families that I have to contact with the tragic news."

"He meant no offense." Tarsik spoke up. "Mr. Ansul processes things a little differently than the rest of us but he meant no disrespect I can assure you."

The minister nodded hesitantly.

"Guards at the morgue?" Tarsik asked.

"No, we don't post security details at the morgue for, obvious reasons. She killed a security officer and a flight technician on pad six before making off with one of our orbital shuttles."

Tarsik's scarred face once again wrinkled into an expression of rage.

"Then she's off-planet?!" he shouted. "How long ago did she break atmo?"

"I received word less than five minutes ago, the shuttle lifted off less than a minute before that. We run an efficient operation Captain."

"Hmmph." Tarsik grumbled and shifted around uncomfortably. He paused, deep in thought. Then, "I have a truly crazy if you'll give it consideration"

The minister seemed hesitant to respond, then shook his head, "Oh no...there is no way I could allow it. Captain you must understand that this is a *most* unusual situation and that until we have it figured out we must..."

"Oh blow it out your exhaust!" Ansul snorted.

Tarsik didn't even consider reprimanding him.

"Excuse me?" the stuffy little prime-worlder scoffed.

Tarsik flapped his cape out of the way, exposing his sidearm, then took several heavy steps toward the minster and his entourage. Weapons raised quickly and came to bear on the large spacer's chest.

"I wouldn't." the doctor stated matter-of-factly to Felize's men.

The minister held up a hand to stay his guards.

"Sir?" one of them asked, his voice muffled by the rayproof helmet that he wore.

"If these two wanted me dead the lot of you would be burned down before you knew what had happened." Felize said, turning to his men, "Rayproof armor or not."

The captain smiled wickedly. He was delighted that his reputation had preceded him. He attempted to soften his glare and then spoke, "Minister I don't mean to be demanding but you have..."

He was cut off by Felize's tele-wave chiming. The minister raised the wrist mounted unit to his face and pressed the button. "Felize, go ahead."

The voice on the other end sounded rather distressed. "Minister there's been...an incident."

"What kind of incident?" he snapped back.

"Sir...we've lost cruiser eighty-three with all hands and cruiser seventeen is drifting and reporting she is on fire."

The minister's face went white. Tarsik could see that the man had never received news so shocking in all of his career. For a moment Tarsik wondered if Ansul was thinking the same thing he was, that they'd blown into town and had brought trouble to these primers the likes of which they'd never seen before.

"I...uh..." the minister stammered.

Tarsik strode up and grabbed the man's wrist, ignoring the rifles that were once again pointed at him. "This is Captain Tarsik of the Service ship *Honshu*. "The cruisers, they were chasing Von Braun's stolen shuttle correct?"

"Yes sir." came the response after a moment of silence.

"They were attacked? What type of ship?"

"Attacked in low orbit...something we've never seen before...we're still trying to determine its origin. It jumped in just outside of atmo and tore the cruisers apart before they knew what had hit them."

Tarsik turned and pointed at Ramus' portable screen. Ansul took the hint and grabbed it from the doctor, turned it over, then read off the number on the back of it. "Three-oh-two."

"Can you route any visual and audio data on the encounter to TSM portable screen number 302?"

"Minister?" came the response.

"Do as he says." Felize commanded.

There was a short delay before the woman on the other end replied, "Sending it through now."

"Thank you Commander." Felize said before wrestling his arm free of Tarsik's grip and deactivating the tele-wave.

Once again he waved his men away and huddled around the screen with Tarsik and the doctor as Ansul brought it forward. The screen flickered and switched over to what appeared to be telemetry data from orbital sensor buoys. The two police cruisers were clearly indicated and seemed to be in close pursuit of the stolen orbital shuttle which was also marked with a designation on the screen. Then, with no warning whatsoever, a red icon appeared on the readout that was marked as "unidentified".

The telemetry disappeared and was quickly replaced with what appeared to be video footage from the telescopic nose camera from cruiser seventeen. The craft was like nothing any of them had seen before. Despite the glare of the setting sun at their backs the screen itself was in the shade of the bodies huddled around it and had plenty enough brightness to make out other craft moving about in orbit but the subject of the video record was difficult to make out.

"She's painted all black." Ansul mumbled under his breath.

The craft was a rocket, that much was certain, but it was angular and coated in a material that was not only nearly as black as the space behind it but also seemed to have a matte quality to its finish.

"Unidentified vessel this is Casidaen System Police

cruiser 17, you are ordered to identify yourself immediately." came the crackly voice of some officer unknown to the *Honshu* men.

The video continued to show the orbital shuttle heading straight for the mysterious craft at high speed. The system police tried twice more to order the vessel to identify herself and prepare for boarding but their hails were met with silence. Then, without any warning whatsoever, the flash of torpedoes being ejected from tubes. The feed gave them a clear view of the torpedoes tearing into the hull of cruiser 83. The audio chatter was interspersed with screaming as the ship broke apart. The crew of 17 started to panic as they attempted to pull away and arm for battle but the feed, both audio and video, went silent a moment later as the flash of an explosion filled the screen.

Ansul handed the screen off to the minister, who seemed to be in shock.

"*Now*," Tarsik asked, "are you ready to consider my crazy idea?"

24\\

"It really doesn't look right in green does it?" Ansul remarked as he and his captain strode up to the towering hulk of the imposter *Honshu*.

"Hmmph." was the only reply Tarsik gave.

The situation was bizarre in the extreme and the captain tried to remind himself that from their perspective *he* and *his crew* were the imposters. Still, it was deeply unsettling to stare oneself in the eye, a feeling that only intensified as they approached and he literally met the gaze of the other Harridor Tarsik. He didn't have the scar on his lip from the barroom brawl on Throntus VI, but the state of his cape, as tattered as his own, and the patch covering the other man's left eye told him that this Tarsik was no less of a stranger to violence.

"Who in the space-blasted hell's crazy idea was this?!" the alternate Tarsik bellowed at them.

The captain raised his hand and gave a sarcastic little half grin.

Eyepatch Tarsik threw his hands up in frustration, "Okay, yeah, this guy is definitely *not* me." and with that he stepped forward and gave Tarsik a good look up and down, "If you were me would you be okay with this? I don't know if I even believe in all of this transdimensional duplicate tark-snipe."

Captain Tarsik rubbed at the back of his neck and let out a soft chuckle, "Well...if you told me a week ago that I was going to slingshot into the distant past and shoot a t-rex in the face I wouldn't have believed that either..." he threw his hands up, "yet...here we are!"

Ansul nodded, "Yes, we have seen some *pretty* crazy shit as of late."

"Who *is* this?" Eyepatch Tarsik growled but was silenced by a look of bewilderment on his counterpart's face as not one, but *two*, Emily Fausts walked down the ramp behind him.

The captain recognized Faust, his Faust, immediately. The other sported much tackier hair and makeup and even carried herself differently. He thought he detected a slight stagger to her walk, one that indicated she had either been drinking or was hungover from drinking.

"Faust?!" he cried out, feeling his voice nearly crack with emotion.

"Yep." she replied plainly. She was still angry, and Tarsik couldn't rightly blame her but regardless he was happy to see that she was okay.

"How did you...?" he shook his head.

"These guys kinda kidnapped me while I was taking my ship out for a test flight." she pointed up to the much smaller craft attached to the side of the green *Honshu*'s hull.

"Casidaen Starworks F-type, nice." Ansul smiled.

"I was wondering what that rust bucket stuck to the side of this funky green *Honshu* was."

"Don't try to crack jokes." Emily snapped at her former captain.

Eyepatch Tarsik looked back at his own Faust and then back to the other Tarsik. "You're a bit um...chummy...is the word I'm looking for, aren't you Captain? I guess whatever life you lived afforded you time to kid around."

suffocating layer of liquid.

"I have decided that my given name shall no longer be spoken. It is time that you all begin to call me by my prophesied name instead."

Von Braun felt a twinge of anger toward the youth. It wasn't enough that she'd been born into a time without war, or a family with enough wealth to control the fates of entire star systems...no, she didn't just want her power to emanate from her wealth...she wanted to be *worshipped* as a goddess.

Tali assuming the role of Deliah had always been the plan, but Essa had thought that the girl's time as a scared inmate on Subterra Prime would have provided her with some humility. She could see now that she'd been wrong about that. Still, being the high priestess of a goddess who ruled over an entire newly terraformed paradise planet was something Von Braun had no intentions of passing over. She'd hoped to have had more time as the commander of Aeolus Station in order to wring some personal profit out of the endeavor, but she would now be joining her mistress on Dathon VII a little earlier thanks to the business with Tarsik and his men.

"Yes," she said in a submissive tone, "I understand Deliah."

Her words were followed by what must have been no less than a ten second silence.

"You know," Tali said, "I have been thinking and I have come to the realization that if I am to be a goddess then those around me should behave as though they are in the presence of one. Don't you think?"

"Mistress?" Von Braun asked, averting her eyes instinctively.

"Kneel, Essa. Kneel before Deliah."

A feeling of pure outrage manifested in Von Braun's consciousness.

"How dare this spoiled little toad speak to me in such a fashion?!" her inner monologue screamed as her lips

25\\

Essa Von Braun strode confidently past the guards outside of Tali Asaddan'fal'fa'falool's quarters. The doors parted with a mechanical whir and she stepped into what appeared at first to be a chamber in total darkness. Within seconds, however, her eyes adjusted and she could see stars outside of the enormous picture window directly across from the door. It was situated just above what she could now make out as a large marble bathing vessel which was flanked by two blue-skinned servants.

"Essa" the words were spoken softly by the young Frazian heiress who was submerged neck deep in what appeared to be an almost opalescent silver/white liquid, "this was most certainly *not* the plan."

"Forgive me Tali I..."

"STOP!" the tiny figure's voiced boomed in the mostly empty room. With that she rose out of the pool, the slightly viscous layer of bathing fluid immediately beginning to cascade down the curves of her mottled skin of blue and yellow. The two servants stepped forward and began to wipe the fluid from her body as she herself wiped some of it from her hair-tendrils which seemed to spread out on their own, as if relieved to be freed from the accompanied those deaths. He hoped, however, that there was still time to mend fences and continue training her as his apprentice.

The alternate Faust had excused herself when the lift had stopped at the level her quarters were on. She'd seemed perfectly content to let the other Emily take over piloting duties for the duration of the mission. Tarsik found that completely out of character, proving that the duplicates couldn't be counted on to act as they would.

As the doors opened everyone piled out and Faust took her place in the pilot's seat, Herschel his place at the operations console, and Ansul sat at the back of the cockpit with Minister Felize. It seemed that everyone had a place, except for the two Tarsiks of course. They bumped into one another as they each vied for position at the captain's console behind the pilot's chair.

"*My* ship." Eyepatch Tarsik roared, "Take a seat at the back!" he said as he shoved a brawny finger toward the rear of the cockpit.

Captain Tarsik gave a quick mock smile and nod and then cocked his large right fist back and swung directly at the other man's jaw. Hilariously however, for Ansul and the minister who had a clear view of proceedings, the alternate Tarsik had apparently had the exact same idea at the exact same time and what resulted was both men punching each other squarely in the face simultaneously. Both of them reeled from the blows and staggered back a step.

They turned at the sound of applause. Ansul had a huge smile on his face and was laughing uncontrollably.

"Not so different after all I guess."

Tarsik's chest swelled and he stepped forward with a furious scowl on his face, ready to knock the imposter onto his ass.

"Gentlemen!" Minister Felize called from behind Ansul. "Forgive me if I'm incorrect here but I believe that at this very moment we have a fugitive that is escaping our grasp. Perhaps we should nix the chit chat and get on with this insanity."

Both captains Tarsik nodded in agreement. Just then a voice called from the top of the ramp, "We're ready to lift at a moment's notice ma'am." he was addressing the alternate Faust.

Tarsik and Ansul's hearts skipped a beat as they looked up to see that the voice belonged to none other than Junior Pilot Herschel.

Noticing their reaction Faust interjected, "Tell me about it. Imagine how *I* reacted when I saw him." she then waved them along, "Come on, we're losing time."

Minister Felize bumped into Ansul as he halted to let the alternate Tarsik board before he did.

"Where do you think you're going Minister?" Tarsik turned and asked him.

"With you of course. Did you really think I was going to agree to releasing these...doppelgangers without direct supervision? We have no idea what we're dealing with and since I'm the one sticking my neck out on this I'd prefer to oversee any reality smashing temporal mayhem myself."

"You have a point, fair enough." Tarsik said as he moved to let the minister board first.

The transport lift from the loading bay to the cockpit was slower than on his *Honshu* Tarsik mentally noted as they rode in silence. He glanced over, quickly so that she wouldn't take notice, at Faust. He thought about what she had said only moments before about her reaction to seeing Herschel alive and well. He knew that she directly blamed herself for his death and having lost people under his command before he knew the intense guilt that unconsciously pursed themselves into an expression of anger, one that she quickly corrected as she kneeled as commanded. A servant approached, hunched over in a submissive posture, and presented Tali with a robe of fine Devrallan silk which she slipped on gracefully.

"You little bitch!" Essa screamed into the abyss of her own mind, "If it weren't for me the felons on Subterra Prime would have eaten you for dinner!"

She was brought back to reality as Tali's feet, still damp with the shiny opalescent bathing liquid, came into view in front of her. The girl stood over Essa and placed one delicate hand onto the older woman's shoulder.

"You were to be my herald, my priestess, she who would stand by my side and attest to my greatness."

"Were?!" Von Braun snapped, lifting her eyes to meet Tali's.

The goddess-to-be bent and brushed the cheek of the fuming human who knelt before her. Without warning she grabbed Essa's jaw and shook it angrily.

"But you just couldn't stick with the program could you Essa?!"
With that she released her grip and turned her back to Von Braun who, in a blind rage, nearly pulled the dagger from her boot and plunged it into the girl's back. She didn't, however, because she knew that would only result in her own death at the hands of Tali's guards. Still, it was tempting.

"Go." Tali's voice echoed in the chamber, her right hand making a dismissive gesture.

Essa gritted her teeth, stood, then turned for the door. As she walked toward it her mind raced with ideas of how she would make the impudent young girl's life a living hell for crossing her.

26\\

Minister Felize had settled the argument between the two captains Tarsik rather quickly. He'd allowed the alternate captain to retain direct command over his ship and crew, but had demanded that the overall mission was under the authority of the Tarsik from his own timeline.

This had mostly brought peace to the cockpit as Captain Tarsik took a seat at the rear alongside the minister and Ansul.

The ship blasted into orbit quite shakily Ansul noted, likely due to the lack of his own perfectionism when it came to the engines. Minister Felize, seeming quite uncomfortable as he gripped the seat harness for dear life, rattled off the authorization codes to Herschel that would allow them to access all of the telemetry collected by orbital satellites.

Once the *Gronshu*, as Ansul had dubbed the green *Honshu*, was comfortably in orbit everyone save for Faust removed their safety harnesses and headed over to Herschel's station. His fingers danced over the clickity-clackity keys as various datasets flashed across the screen. There were over 1000 satellites in orbit of Tersis that had collected data on the intruder and they intended to know what they were up against.

A moment later Herschel had ceased typing furiously at the keyboard but the computer took a few moments to catch up to his input. Screens flashed by in rapid succession until finally it stopped on one particular readout; a composite diagram of the enigmatic ship.

"You have got to be kidding me." Ansul mumbled under his breath from behind his captain.

"Your Martian is right," Eyepatch Tarsik said to his counterpart, "she's a beast."

"Two hundred and fifty-centimeter armor...at least!" Herschel read off nervously, "twelve torpedo launchers, thirty-two proton beam arrays, fifty point defense proton turrets, and a drive...well I've never seen anything with such power before."

"Well, at least she's still using proton weapons." Eyepatch Tarsik scoffed.

"Still?!" Ansul snipped.

"The alternate Tarsik nodded, "Yeah, she's obviously not upgraded to lepton banks."

"And this ship is, I assume?" Tarsik asked.

"Of course," his doppelganger snarled, "I take pride in keeping the *Honshu* as up to date as I can and I sure as space-blasted hell wouldn't want to take her into battle with substandard armament."

"What the captain is trying to say," Ansul chimed in, "is that in this reality there's no such thing as lepton banks, at least not yet."

"Hmmph," the eyepatched spacer rubbed his chin, "well, at least if we have to engage them we have superior weaponry."

"Superior perhaps," came the voice of Yatin Ramus who'd entered the cockpit only few moments before, "but we're still heavily outgunned." he shook his head looking at the readout on the computer screen, "I haven't seen anything like that monster since the war."

"The war?" Herschel and his captain asked in unison.

"It's a very long story," explained Tarsik, "but Doctor Ramus here we've recently learned is a relic from the Colonial Wars. He's seen true warships with his own eyes, so I'd listen to what he has to say."

Ramus smiled, turned to his captain, "Harry," he said, uncharacteristically using such a familiar moniker, "I think it may be time to call in some old favors."

Looking through the collected data further it became clear that the doctor was right. The *Gronshu* wouldn't last long in a firefight with the stealth ship. Captain Tarsik excused himself to the briefing room to place some waves to a few old friends while Herschel and Ansul set themselves upon the task of determining where the bogey had fled to. Attempting to ascertain an NC trajectory was, under normal circumstances, virtually impossible. The wealth of data from Tersis' satellites, however, made it a feasible though still quite daunting task.

It took nearly ten minutes for the two to devise an algorithm to process the data and the *Gronshu's* computer had been plugging away at the data for nearly another ten minutes before the door opened and Captain Tarsik once again strode into the cockpit.

"Any luck?" Ansul asked.

"Some," he said in a mildly irritated tone, "Exactly how much is going to depend on where it is we're going to confront this thing."

As if it were listening to the conversation and attempting to interject at just the right moment the ship's computer beeped and the display switched to a star chart.

"Well I'll be damned." Eyepatch Tarsik laughed.

"You recognize the place?" Ansul asked.

"Damned right. We were just there. That's Dathon VII!"

Tarsik furrowed his brow in thought for a moment then spoke, "If that's our heading then there's only two ships that are going to be in range to help. One is the *Mudskipper*..."

Ansul cut him off, smiling broadly, "Rannigan! Haven't seen him in a while."

The eyepatched Tarsik jumped in, "You know Rannigan too? I guess our lives aren't *completely* different after all."

The captain gave a little half-grin and continued, "The other is...ugh I can't believe I'm having to say this...it's the *Redmane*."

"Kurian?!" both Ansul and the alternate Tarsik blurted out, then turned to each other with a knowing look of disapproval.

"I can see," Tarsik said, "that by the look on your face Kurian is as big of an asshole in your timeline as he is in ours."

"To put it lightly." the doppelganger growled, raking his fingers over his eye patch.

A look of shock came over the captain's face. He reached up and felt the scar that was mostly hidden behind his left eyebrow.

"Knife fight in a bar, Kentaurus IIIB." he stated but it was obviously a question.

"Yes how did you..." Eyepatch began, but then came to the same realization as his counterpart.

"It would seem," Doctor Ramus spoke up, "that some of the differences between our two realities are little more than, well, skin deep as it were."

27\\

Many shall dash themselves against the rocks of fate. Their bodies the kindling upon which the fire of Deliah's coming shall burn. The great tumult of humanity, their pained cries and lamentations the trumpet that heralds her arrival. A new day shall be born from the ashes of destruction as the parched soil is quenched by the blood of the people. The clouds shall yield to sunlight and the memory of dust shall fade into history, replaced by the verdant plains of Deliah's glory.

- translated from the Testament of the Prophet Joachim, year 0 B.R.

28\\

Before departing the Casidaen system something had occurred to Ansul. Just who would have the resources to construct a ship like the stealth vessel that had jumped into Tersis space? There were broad ranging implications for everyone in the Federated Worlds if someone was building ships the likes of which had not been seen since the Colonial Wars.

On a hunch he'd quickly remoted in to *Honshu*'s systems and downloaded what information he could from their encounter with the *Prometheus*. Tarsik had stood over his shoulder at one of the auxiliary consoles, intermittently bracing for NC jumps, as the Martian performed his comparison. The evidence was almost incontrovertible; the stealth dreadnought's neutron drive signature matched *Prometheus'* almost perfectly. Whatever the mystery ship was up to it had been designed and built by Interplanetary Holdings!

"One more skip to Dathon VII." Faust called out.

The others braced themselves for the familiar sensation of NC travel. There was the usual flash of light and spiral of color, the sudden sinking feeling in the pit of the stomach, and then Dathon VII filled the forward facing portions of the cockpit windows. In space size is not always the easiest thing to judge from a distance but the utter chaos of the planet's atmosphere, with dozens if not hundreds or large storms visible moving about its surface, gave the impression that Dathon VII was a bit larger than most inhabited worlds. Everyone in the cockpit crowded forward to get a better look. Then, against the backdrop of the hazy mustard-tinged atmosphere Ansul's eyes picked out something that didn't belong.

"What in space-blasted hell is that?" he cried out.

"What?" Tarsik asked.

"That, right there!" he pointed to a spot along the day/night terminator.

Many pairs of eyes scanned the sky where the Martian claimed to see something but it was a moment before anyone else saw what Ansul's dark-adapted eyes were able to make out. Doctor Ramus was the first to see it, though it took several seconds for his brain to make sense of what it was he was seeing.

"By the Great Galactic Serpent..." he mumbled to himself but so quiet was the cockpit that everyone present clearly heard his words.

"That's..." Faust started.

"...a fraggin genesis engine!" the alternate Tarsik cut her off.

The shape was unmistakable. Floating only a few hundred kilometers over the planet's surface its distinctive silhouette, akin to an enormous spaceborne lotus flower, stood in stark contrast to the atmosphere below.

"I don't see it." Fizril said in disappointed fashion.

Ansul pulled the big cat closer to him and held out his arm and pointed directly at the object.

"I still do not see it." Fizril growled.

"It's okay Crewman." the doctor assured him, "Antarian eyes are not as sharp as human ones at long distances, and certainly not as advanced as Martian eyes."

"Hmmph." Fizril grumbled. He turned away from the

cockpit windows and gave them a dismissing gesture, "They are better than *either* of yours at detecting motion though."

Having no interest in engaging in a conversation about ocular evolution eyepatch Tarsik turned to Herschel, "Those things require large quantities of elorite to function, correct?"

"Yes Sir." the junior pilot acknowledged.

"Explains the runs we've been making then."

"Care to enlighten us?" Captain Tarsik asked his counterpart.

"We've been delivering some pretty sizeable loads of elorite to this place for a while now. Had no idea what they planned to do with it but they made it worth our while so we didn't ask questions."

Shaking his head the regular Tarsik scolded his doppelganger, "It's also pretty damned unstable and usually requires skirting a few laws to get hold of. I would never endanger my crew in such a fashion and I definitely wouldn't risk the seizure of my ship over a shady contract."

"Look here," Eyepatch deepened his tone and his brow furrowed in anger, "my people know exactly what they're in for. I don't hide a damned thing from them, and the last time I checked elorite is not an illegal material to transport. Just because you're too afraid to take some minor risks to grow your business..."

"Grow my business?!" Tarsik snarled, "A couple of proton blasts from a pirate ship and this green monstrosity you call the *Honshu* would have been vaporized! And don't get me started on legality. Elorite might not be outright illegal but you know as well as I do that the majority of what's on the market comes from Jenthik worlds and that the mining of it has serious and long-lasting consequences for their environments."

The alternate captain broke out into a chuckle, "Maybe you and I are more different than we are alike.

Look I'm no big fan of the Jenthik poisoning the few planets capable of supporting them by mining the stuff but if they're that short-sighted who am I to tell them to stop?"

Faust had been keeping up with the politics surrounding elorite in intergalactic news and knew very well that many systems had banned its sale, especially if it could be traced back to a Jenthik colony world, but she knew it was not the time or place for such a discussion. She stood up from the pilot's seat and grabbed the overhead mic that hung above the captain's console. With the push of a few buttons she shut off the feed to the rest of the ship and routed the output only to the cockpit speakers.

"Enough!" she yelled into it, causing everyone present to flinch at the pure volume of her voice. She waited for all of them to turn to her before she continued, "Are we going to act like children or are we going to do what we came here to do?"

No one dared respond. The scowl on her face left even the two Tarsiks speechless.

"There's a stealth ship out there that has us dead to rights if it gets the jump on us! Anyone want to be on the receiving end of that dreadnought's firepower?"

In a manner reminiscent of small children that had been corrected by a teacher all of the men shook their heads.

"That's what I thought." she said, this time without the microphone button pressed.

Minister Felize leaned in to Crewman Jones and whispered, "Maybe I should have insisted that *she* be in charge." to which Jones chuckled to himself.

"Emily you're right," Tarsik spoke up, "We need to locate that ship." he turned to Herschel, "Junior Pilot are our scanners picking up anything that could be a vessel?"

"Excuse me?!" Eyepatch bellowed.

"Sirs..." Herschel interjected but his voice was lost in

the shouting.

"You may have forgotten that this is my ship and that I'm the one who issues orders in this cockpit."

"Sirs..." Herschel tried again.

"Oh no," regular Tarsik replied, "I didn't forget." he shook his head and gave a snide grin, "But *I'm* the commander of this mission and that gives me..."

"Sirs..."

"Don't even try that!" the alternate captain yelled at his counterpart, "We are in space and..."

"SIRS!!!" Herschel shouted over their blustering. Both turned to see a look of terror on the junior pilot's face, then he broke from his momentary fear of being reprimanded, "We have incoming!

The two captains, now silent, could hear the beep-beeping of the scanners tracking a torpedo. Instinctively the alternate Tarsik rushed over to man his station behind the pilot's chair and, without really thinking, regular Tarsik hurried Minister Felize, Jones, and Fizril to the seats at the back of the cockpit and they all strapped in.

"Time to impact?" the captain asked.

"Fifteen seconds." Herschel replied.

"Pilot, maximum burn!"

29\\

"I'll give it to them they're more skilled than I would have thought Service rabble to be." Captain Hadant muttered to himself aboard the stealth dreadnought as the *Honshu* deftly evaded their torpedo and took it out with a hail of point-defense fire. "Are there any indications that they've detected us?" he asked the array of crewmen who were manning their bridge stations.

"Negative Sir." a young human female at the operations console responded.

"Good." Hadant said, leaning back into the captain's chair. "Prepare tubes seven through twelve. Let's see how well they handle an entire salvo."

"Playing, are we Ferricus?" came a voice from behind him.

The captain turned to see Tali Asaddan'fal'fa'falool standing in the doorway. He got to his feet quickly and immediately went into a small bow.

"Mistress..." he said, "I believe they've come looking for Ms. Von Braun. I thought them to the perfect test subject to determine the true capabilities of this ship since they pose no real threat to us."

"Hmm." Tali sighed and then hesitated, watching in

delight as the Glintarin awkwardly maintained his bow. Even in the incredibly dim lighting of the *Calypso's* bridge she could clearly see beads of sweat running down the man's forehead. "It's okay Captain, continue," she said nonchalantly, "but I wish to observe."

"Of course mistress." he said, then after a quick respectful nod of the head returned to his chair.

"Status of tubes seven through twelve?" he asked.

"Tubes loaded Captain. Ready to fire on your mark."

Ferricus Hadant could feel the spines on the back of his head begin to prick up as he felt the looming presence of Tali Asaddan'fal'fa'falool. The child-turned-goddess, had walked forward to stand menacingly over him. Her physical presence was anything but, however Hadant knew that the future of his warship project hung on the amity of her father.

"Very well. Fire tubes seven through twelve."

There was the slightest hint of vibration in the deck plates as six twenty-five megaton atomic warheads were hurled free of their tubes by compressed nitrogen gas. The bridge's main screen was still displaying a magnified image of the pathetic little green Service rocket. Hadant watched as the main drive plume of their target once again flared and within seconds the engine trails of the torpedoes became visible on the screen as well.

"Got you now." he muttered under his breath but he'd spoken too soon. Point defense fire from the *Honshu* took out one of the torpedoes as they closed in and just when it seemed that the remaining five would strike their target down the aged Service rocket vented an unusually large amount of maneuvering thruster propellant out of her belly and climbed several hundred meters on the z axis in less than a second. Two of the torpedoes collided with one another. Their shockwave appeared to damage the guidance system of one of the other remaining torpedoes as it suddenly shot off wildly in what looked like a totally random direction.

The *Honshu* herself looked to have caught a bit of the shockwave, as her aft section heaved was tossed and a few small pieces of debris seemed to float free of the ship.

"Status?!" Eyepatch cried out as he struggled to right himself, having nearly fallen to the deck during the buffeting the *Gronshu* had endured.

"Fin three is showing significant structural damage, but otherwise we're green all across the board Sir." Herschel called back.

"Jones...err...Faust, cut our engines. Make it look like we've lost power."

Emily hesitated for only the briefest of instances before reminding herself that eye patch or no this was still Captain Tarsik and she trusted that he knew what he was doing.

"Engines off, Aye." she called out as she pulled the throttle back to zero.

From the rear of the cockpit Captain Tarsik could only bite his lip. He knew that even the slightest distraction could prove fatal, especially when fighting an enemy so well armed and so difficult to detect.

"Two remaining torpedoes are re-acquiring target Captain." Herschel announced.

"Mmm hmm." the ship's commander grunted his acknowledgement.

The beeping of the bogeys on scanners steadily grew more rapid as they began homing in on the now coasting *Gronshu*. The air was deathly still in the cockpit and Tarsik felt as though he could hear the sound of his own heartbeat pounding in his ears. It took every bit of restraint that he possessed not to jump to his feet and begin calling out orders.

"Herschel," eye patch Tarsik spoke softly, "prepare tactical maneuver theta two."

"Theta two?" regular Tarsik thought to himself, "What the space-blasted hell is maneuver theta two?!"

"On my mark...", the alternate captain instructed, "hold...hold...now Herschel!"

On the *Calypso's* screen the *Honshu* looked like a goner and Captain Hadant permitted himself a smile.

"Two seconds to impact..." the operations officer called out.

Without warning a large amount of debris seemed to be ejected from *Honshu's* aft section. They had blown the doors off of the loading bay and had vented atmosphere!

"Hang on!!!" Tarsik screamed.

The deceptive silence of space belied the ferocity of the fifty megaton explosion that detonated less than half a kilometer behind the *Gronshu*. The resulting shockwave flattened her rear fins into the fuselage and compressed the cargo bay well into the aft section of the ship.

The impact was far too much for the gravity generators to cancel out. Poor Fizril, who had not had time to adjust the safety harness on his seat to match his height, and was therefore wearing only the lap belt, was shaken so violently that as his upper body was thrown about his head came back and struck the bulkhead with enough force to knock him unconscious.

The lights flickered in the cockpit and then dropped to black as Eyepatch, steadfastly holding onto the grips he'd installed above the captain's console, felt the gravity switch off. Once, twice, the lights tried to come back to life but flickered out again. Finally after what felt like an eternity, but was in reality likely no more than ten or fifteen seconds they came on again and this time they stayed on.

Minister Felize jumped with a start as he saw Fizril's face right next to his, blood droplets floating from both nostrils. A moment later the gravity kicked in and the big cat fell limp. Pushing past his own fragility the doctor unfastened his harness with lightning speed and moved to attend to the wounded Antarian.

"Jones, Minister, help!" he shouted.

The two men did as instructed without any sign of hesitation.

"Status?" the captain asked, looking around to survey the situation on the bridge.

Herschel called back, "The rear fins and the loading bay they're...they're *gone* sir!" his console beeped and he tapped a few keys. New information filled his screen. "It looks like two out of three engines are still functional, but we're getting casualty reports from all decks."

"That's it." Yatin barked, "I'll be in the medical bay assisting my counterpart." and then to Felize and Jones, indicating Fizril "Help me get him to the lift."

Hadant felt the air leave the room. All around him subordinates were throwing anxious glances at one another. Behind him he heard the spoiled Frazian girl stir. He expected a chiding but instead only heard the rustle of cloth as her fingers dug into the small velvet purse that she kept on her belt. She brought the fingers up to her nose and sniffed at the sparkling silver and green dust that covered them, mindshade.

Ferricus assumed that she'd become addicted during her time on Subterra Prime, a form of self-soothing to stave off the madness that such a place could induce. He wondered, however, if the coping mechanism itself had created the schism in her psyche that now allowed her to think herself divine?

He shook away the thoughts and returned his attention to the present. "Tubes one through six, load with one-hundred megaton atomics and fire when ready."

"Aye sir." the operations officer acknowledged.

Hadant's spines once again pricked up as he felt Tali lean in behind him to whisper in his ear.

"I know that you're having fun with this monstrosity that you've constructed Captain, but I am much more concerned with the completion of our plan. Destroy them now. That's an order."

"That is precisely what I intend to do Mistress." he responded in the most stoic tone he could muster.

A harsh klaxon sounded from one of the wall consoles to Hadant's left and one of the bridge crew, a Rigellian man named Larvan, ran over to press the button that was flashing red.

"Captain the docking bay is signaling that we have an unauthorized shuttle launch."

"What?" Ferricus demanded. "Who's aboard it?!"

Another alert sound from the operations console drew their attention.

"Incoming wave from the shuttle Captain."

"Put it through!"

The speakers above crackled to life and the voice of Essa Von Braun came over them. "Captain Hadant, I need you to relay a message for me to Mistress Deliah."

"No need." the Frazian said authoritatively.

There was a short silence. It was apparent that Von Braun had not anticipated Tali's presence on the bridge.

"Mistress." she responded over tele-wave, "I have decided that I and I alone should proceed to the station to initiate the terraforming process."

"You what?!" Tali roared, her eyes glowing with anger and her words barely escaping clenched teeth. "I am Deliah! I am the one to remake Dathon VII! Not you, you presumptuous..."

"Mistress!" Essa seemed to plead to be heard. "I am

the one that failed you. Therefore I am the one who should take the risk, not you!"

"The risk?" Tali replied, gazing up toward the speakers as if Von Braun could see her, her face still twisted in anger.

"Yes Mistress. Elorite is unstable and the genesis engine is still highly experimental. I would rather sacrifice my life than yours should anything go wrong."

Tali stood in silence for a moment. It was apparent that Essa had stumbled upon something that she had not considered.

"Very well..." she said, greatly subduing her tone of voice, "but know that accepting this risk on my behalf will *not* guarantee your reinstatement as my high priestess."

"If only she could see me smiling." Essa thought to herself. "Stupid little bitch." then aloud, "Of course Mistress. It is a risk that I undertake of my own accord."

"Good." the goddess-to-be replied, "Then get on with it." and with that she gestured for the tele-wave to be terminated.

Hadant was staring at the small display in the arm of his captain's chair that he'd switched over to show torpedo tube status. He allowed himself only the smallest hint of a smile as he saw the final tube light up red to indicate that it was loaded and prepared to fire.

"Firing tubes one through six."

Like before the rocket trails appeared on the main viewer as the torpedoes screamed toward their target. One of the *Honshu's* point-defense turrets sprang to life but it was apparent that most of them were inoperable. The bridge crew of the *Calypso* watched as two of the Service ship's engines fired to life.

"No escape this time." Hadant thought to himself.

Just then the visual of the *Honshu* on the main display shrunk to a picture-in-picture size as half of the screen filled with a telemetry readout.

"Two new contacts Captain." the scanner operator

said.

Hadant jumped to his feet, "What?!"

Surely enough two silhouettes appeared on the telemetry readout. He glanced back at the *Honshu* visual and his heart sank as the picture window lit up with bright proton cannon fire as the six torpedoes blinked out of existence one after the other.

30\\

"Yes!" Ansul cheered as the bogeys were reduced to brief white hot flashes of light. "I never thought I'd be happy to see Kurian but here we are." he joked.

"I couldn't agree more." Tarsik beamed.

His eyepatched counterpart turned to both of them with a stern look, "Can we save the celebration for later, when we're decidedly *not* dead?"

"Captain I think I've got something you're going to want to see!" Herschel interjected.

The captain quickly made his way over to the operations console which was currently flashing with more warning lights and making a larger bevy of sounds than he'd ever seen or heard before.

"Captain I've got incoming waves from both the *Mudskipper* and the *Redmane*." Faust announced.

Eyepatch turned to his doppelganger and motioned for him to answer the hails, and then to the pilot, "Keep a sharp eye out, I doubt they're out of torpedoes."

"Aye Sir." she responded, her focus never leaving the instrument readouts.

"What is it Junior Pilot?" the captain asked as he dropped to a knee next to Herschel's chair.

"This tele-wave was intercepted during the fight."

He handed his headset over to his captain, so that he might hear over the background conversation between the other Tarsik, Rannigan, and that scoundrel Kurian. The captain listened to the entire message and then handed the headset back to Herschel.

"That wasn't encrypted." Eyepatch stated emphatically.

"No sir." he knew it wasn't a question but still felt as though he needed to respond.

The captain rubbed his temples, "She *wanted* us to hear that."

And with that he stood and went back to his console. His counterpart and the Martian had just wrapped up their conversation with the two other Service captains.

"Pilot, any eyes on that stealth ship?"

"Negative Captain." Faust replied, then "The *Redmane* caught a glimpse of something on scanners when she dropped out of NC. Both ships fired on it and they detected a couple of hits but then it moved off. They're still searching."

He looked over at his duplicate who nodded in agreement with the pilot's report. His eyes shifted around the room and he rubbed at his temples again before speaking, "Junior Pilot do we still have NC capability?" he asked.

The three outsiders in his cockpit immediately burst into statements of objection. They were all talking over one another. The captain gritted his teeth and slammed his fist down onto his console, "Enough! This is *my* ship and *my* crew and we're not sacrificing everything for some job contract that *you* made." he pointed to the other Tarsik angrily. "Junior Pilot," he said through clenched teeth, "do we have NC capability?"

"Yes Sir." came Herschel's response.

The captain paused for a moment in thought and then looked around the room before coming to a decision.

"I'm sorry Captain," he said to his mirror image, "you

know you would do the same thing if you were in my place."

Tarsik wanted so badly to object, to claim authority over the mission as a whole and even relieve his counterpart of command...but he was right. The *Gronshu* was heavily damaged and he was sure that there were already several dead crew members as well as many more injured. He wasn't sure whether or not IPH would honor their commitment to fixing the *Honshu* if he returned without Von Braun, but he couldn't rightfully ask this other Harridor Tarsik to sacrifice his ship and his crew.

"Okay." was all that he said as he gave an understanding little nod.

"Harry, really? We just give up?" Ansul blurted.

"Yeah." Faust replied without turning her head. "We have to Ansul, it's not worth the risk."

Ansul rubbed at the wispy white fur on his face and head furiously, "That just doesn't seem like *us,* you know? We *always* go for broke, it's what we do."

"Ansul," Tarsik said, putting a hand on his first mate's shoulder, "it's over. As long as she's aboard that dreadnought we'll be gambling way too many lives to try to take her."

"Shit." Eyepatch thought to himself, remembering the message from Von Braun that he'd just listened to. He let out a long and pained sigh, "She's uh...she's not on the dreadnought anymore."

"What?!" Tarsik, Ansul and Faust chimed in unison.

"Herschel, play them the message."

The junior pilot pulled the recording from the ship's data-tapes and routed the audio through the cockpit speakers. By the time it had finished playing Faust was out of her seat and facing her captain. She looked as though she had something to say but as per usual Ansul was the first to speak, "Yeah, anyone willing to take a bet on whether or not she's actually going there to activate that thing, or to blow it up out of spite? I don't know if any of you noticed but it sounds like someone's got a god complex and Essa is not the kind to be outdone in the narcissism category."

"My ship!" Faust blurted out.

Both Tarsiks stared her down.

"We take my ship," she said with a sigh, "that way this *Honshu* can get out of danger before it's too late and we can still go after Von Braun."

"I'm sorry," her Tarsik started, "but did I miss something? The last time I checked you weren't exactly *with* us anymore." indicating himself and Ansul. He then immediately caught himself and realized that he was being an ass. "Emily I'm sorry." he said, "I'm just...I'm sorry okay?"

"Mmm hmm." she hummed, running her tongue over her teeth and shifting her feet a bit nervously. "Yeah. Yeah, we're good."

It was obvious to all that they weren't really "good" but the fact that both of them had put aside their egos for a greater cause was a positive first step.

"I hate to be the wet blanket here," Eyepatch tossed in, "but your FTL module is still floating around the Casidaen system. Even if you make it past that dreadnought and catch or kill, whatever I'm not judging, Von Braun, you'll still be stuck in-system without a way back to Tersis."

"Do you think you could wake up that drunken excuse for a pilot you've got?" Emily smirked, "Who knows, maybe the ship getting half shaken apart sobered her up a bit."

"What are you thinking?" Eyepatch asked.

"You and the Gron...*Honshu*...NC to a point a few light-minutes outside of this system and wait for our signal. You're the only ship with external docking clamps to give the *Feather* a ride back to Tersis. In the meantime we might be able to convince Rannigan and Kurian to run a little interference for us so that dreadnought doesn't atomize us the moment we undock."

Neither of the captains Tarsik could find fault with her logic.

31\\

Amid the deafening howl of skimmer engines and dust that seemed to tear at the fabric of his clothing and seek any gap through which it could get into his eyes Taman was still very conscious of the beating of his own heart in his ears. He had fought with the men of other tribes before, but only small and relatively brief conflicts, typically nothing more than five or ten men with blades or projectile shooters scuffling over a newly discovered well or posturing over territorial borders.

This was something entirely different. Such a tangled mass of men and machines, the sky above so clouded with dust from the launch of the heralds and the whizzing of skimmers that it had begun to call down lightning from the clouds themselves. The static electricity was almost palpable, as small plumes of St. Elmo's Fire erupted from the hilts of swords and from the handlebars of skimmers.

No less than a hundred men and women, or perhaps closer to one-hundred and fifty, had descended on Taman and his men amongst the rocky outcroppings that served as something of a natural defensive barrier for the village's eastern edge. He'd watched in horror as Janan, his lieutenant and husband to his sister, had been torn apart by the first barrage of projectile fire, his limp body falling to the sand, almost unrecognizable.

Utilizing the five proton rifles that they had purchased from the outworlders Taman and his men had managed to regroup and quickly disable about half of the attack skimmers just in time for their own to join the battle. He could discern only one enemy that seemed to have an energy weapon, a large man whose clothing was stained with a scarlet pigment and who wore upon his head the skull of a borra-dragon. That would be Gorjiin of the Shandra Tribe, their sheikh's son and heir to the title. He was a man of very little brain but with an abundance of brawn and incredible hostility.

As the skimmers zipped over them they dropped crudely fashioned bombs and incendiary devices into the crags of the outcroppings in an attempt to drive Taman and his men out from their defensive positions. The defenders took pot shots at the skimmers and drivers. This went on for several minutes. Taman's men had little trouble avoiding the attacks, for the most part, but also had much more difficulty in hitting the fast moving targets that whizzed by overhead.

He soon became aware that the survivors of the wrecked skimmers, those that they had easily disabled with proton fire as they had charged the outcroppings, were regrouping and attempted to flank them from the left side. Their own skimmer drivers seemed to notice this as well and a couple of them attempted to break formation and route the enemies who were now on foot. Two, three, four of the attackers fell to the hail of projectile fire from Taman's skimmers but one man signaled for the others to drop to the ground. He ran forward, taking several hits but not falling, and then reached for something in the satchel that he carried over his left shoulder.

"No!" Taman screamed in the direction of his skimmer drivers but they could not hear him. As they approached the man, one of them ready to remove his head from his body with a force-blade, the man detonated whatever was inside the heavy looking satchel. Dust, rocks, and shrapnel pelted Taman and his men as well as the attacking skimmers overhead, one of which lost control and came crashing down into the crags. When he looked up the new sheikh saw only a smoldering hole where the man and two skimmers had been.

Furious, he scrambled from safety amid the crags, wedged his proton rifle firmly into his shoulder, and began firing off bolts into the sea of dust and debris swirling all about them. He could catch only the faintest of glimpses of the skimmers but it was enough. He hit the aft stabilizers of one of them which caused it to lurch violently in his direction. Despite the limited visibility and heavy dress of the pilot Taman was certain that he could see terror in the man's eyes as he plowed ahead with no control straight into a volley of proton blasts. The first two shots hit the driver in the chest and neck, killing him, with the third and fourth shots aimed at the skimmer itself. Taman succeeded, apparently, with the fourth shot to disable the nega-grav generator and the skimmer fell to a crashing halt only meters in front of him.

He turned back, signaled for Atta and Davress to join him, and they made for the cover of the crashed skimmer. Davress was quick and nimble, she threw herself to the ground next to Taman but Atta was not so lucky. The skimmer belonging to Gorjiin swung out of the torrent of dust and the with a single fluid motion the large man ran an improvised spear through Atta's chest with tremendous force, so much that it knocked him back several feet and he fell, impaled to the ground below him.

Taman lined up a shot at one of Gorjiin's aft stabilizers and squeezed the trigger but much to his horror Davress darted in front of his rifle to tend to the fallen Atta. His shot tore through her right side.

"Davress!" he called and immediately dropped the weapon to the ground.

Despite passing through her body, however, the shot had enough energy remaining to carry on to its intended target and Gorjiin was forced to jump free of his skimmer as it careened straight into the swirling mass of dust spiraling around the crags. There was a violent explosion as it collided with another skimmer. Taman registered it in the back of his thoughts, hoped that it had been one of Gorjiin's skimmers and not one of his own defenders.

Taman clawed frantically at Davress' coverings until he found the wound. It was bleeding badly but he immediately recognized that it had, thankfully, been little more than a glancing blow. He was unsure just how deep it had been, thought that he might have damaged her liver to some degree, but knew that in the short term at least she should be okay. He yelled at and signaled his men to come and attend to the wounded. A quick battlefield cauterization of Davress' wound would probably save her life, but he was almost certain that the spear Atta had taken to the chest had pierced the man's heart.

He looked up and wiped at the lenses of his goggles. Dust had adhered to them thanks to the fine spray of blood from the accident with Davress. His eyes caught motion. Gorjiin, the Shandra Tribe colossus, was racing out of the dust storm directly toward him, a large force-blade axe held high over his head. Taman fumbled in the dust for the rifle he had dropped only a moment before but it was already covered over with dust and sand. Then, as if it were nothing short of divine intervention, a bolt of lightning shot down from the maelstrom above and struck the metal hilt of Gorjiin's uplifted force-blade.

"Yadra thou deliverest me from death so that I might witness the coming of Deliah!" the young sheikh shouted through the layers of cloth protecting his face from the storm. Then, turning to his men in the crags and motioning them to rush forward he cried out, "For the new world to come fight and die with me!"

32\\

Bravely they marched forth through air too dark to see and winds too loud to hear, secure in the knowledge that though their bodies might be pierced or broken their immortal spirits would sustain them in this world until the last enemy had fallen and a paradise descended upon them.

- translated from the Testament of the Prophet Joachim, year 0 B.R.

33\\

"Rannigan you ass, I thought you said you had us covered!" Emily Faust shouted into her headset.
"My mistake?" Cal Rannigan, captain of the R.S. *Mudskipper*, replied in a jocular tone over the tele-wave.
"Yeah well one more mistake like that and we'll be toast."
"Aww, you should give yourself more credit Faust. You can outmaneuver anything that dreadnought can throw your way, I know you can."
The mistake the pilot was referring to was Rannigan's lack of thoroughly covering the *Feather* as she separated from the *Gronshu*. The dreadnought had given them a few minutes of peace but had apparently used that time to maneuver around to attack from another angle. It distinctly felt like they were being used as test subjects by the crew of the dreadnought; evaluating her offensive and defensive capabilities.
A full salvo of twelve torpedoes had surprised the whole lot of them the moment the *Feather* undocked from the *Gronshu* and it was only thanks for her excellent piloting skills that Faust was able to keep two of the beasts that were hot on her tail at bay long enough for the others to target and destroy them. Far too close for her comfort,

especially considering that the *Feather* had no defenses of her own.

"Yeah," she replied, "let's not take that chance again though eh?"

"You got it sister."

Faust slammed the small ship's rockets to full burn and they quickly shot away from the other three. Tarsik, sitting behind Emily in the narrow cockpit adjusted the small viewer that protruded from the wall on an adjustable mount and switched it to a rear-facing visual. The *Gronshu*, the *Redmane* and the *Mudskipper* were shrinking away rapidly but he fingered the controls that would force the camera to automatically adjust the zoom so that he could continue to watch the goings on. He was waiting anxiously for the other *Honshu* to get under way and NC out of the fight. Ansul had stayed behind to assist in repairs and to help their engineer verify that the drive was good to go. Jones, Doctor Ramus, and the injured Fizril were also aboard that ship. Tarsik certainly wanted to see the alternate ship and crew escape alive but more than anything he fretted for his own men who were aboard the nearly crippled vessel.

Small flashes of light. Three torpedoes. No, five! The *Redmane's* neutron plume roared to life as she maneuvered to target the projectiles and the much more agile *Mudskipper* simply spun on its axis with thrusters. Proton cannon fire filled the screen and one after the other Tarsik watched as the torpedoes disappeared into flashes of light.

"Why in the space-blasted hell is that thing only firing torpedoes?" he thought to himself. Despite packing one hell of a punch torpedoes weren't typically all that useful against rocketships with operational point-defense turrets or even a particularly maneuverable one with fixed cannons. You didn't generally go around wasting them in such a fashion. It was a much better tactic to wait and use them against a ship that had lost power or against something more stationary like an asteroid base. Then, it came to him. He snatched the tele-wave mic that hung over his seat and made sure the channel was encrypted. "Tarsik to *Mudskipper*, do you copy?"

There was a brief moment of static before the mechanical voice of the ship's copilot, B9, acknowledged receipt of the message.

"You're the fastest thing out there, I want you to immediately turn toward the origin point of those torpedoes and take a run at it."

This time Rannigan was the one to respond, "Are you out of your mind? Worst case scenario we fly straight into a fresh salvo of atomics, best case we crash right into the damned dreadnought itself!"

"Listen, pull off at the last minute. Just trust me. The dreadnought isn't firing her cannons because the residual radiation, although miniscule, would still be enough to show up on scanners for a few seconds."

"Hah," Rannigan laughed, "like a glowing hot gun barrel in the dark of night."

"Exactly!" Tarsik almost jumped in his seat, "They won't risk atomics if you're on a collision course, they'll target you with their cannons instead..."

"And that'll light them right up." Cal finished.

"The *Mudskipper* has an EM shield if I recall, right?"

"Yes sir, and she'll take the first few shots with no damage to the hull. We'll just have to turn ass and run like hell but that'll give Kurian a chance to hit 'em with everything he's got."

There was a crackle in the line and a familiar voice, Tarsik's own, spoke. "This is the *Honshu*, if Rannigan can get that dreadnought to register on scanners we've got a surprise for it."

"Negative." Tarsik shot back, "You need to use the opportunity to get underway, clear of the fighting."

His own voice chuckled wickedly back it him over the tele-wave. "I don't have any plans on sticking around to get blown up. Let's just say it'll be our parting gift."

THE YESTERDAY DILEMMA

Tarsik thought about it and decided that if there was anyone he could trust it *should* be himself. He acknowledged and advised them all to proceed.

The *Mudskipper*, which had been flying defensive patterns around the badly damaged *Honshu* flipped once more on its axis and her eight neutron rockets flared to maximum intensity.

"What in the...?!" Hadant began almost silently but then shouted, "Thrusters hard to starboard!"

"We won't clear in time Captain." the helmsman called back.

"Cannons! All cannons open fire!"

From their vantage point hundreds of kilometers away Captain Tarsik and Pilot Emily Faust watched as red streaks struck out from the darkness of space. The *Mudskipper* appeared to take several direct hits as their energy being deflected by the EM shield caused a momentary shimmer along the ship's hull. Just as they'd planned Rannigan spun the antiquated but nimble little craft about and beat a hasty retreat. Tarsik could only imagine the grin on Kurian's face as he gave the order to fire on the stealth ship. Kurian was a jackal, far more devious and belligerent than even Essa Von Braun, but also a fair share more sane.

The *Redmane* was armed similarly to Tarsik's *Honshu*; not a warship but far from toothless. Her forward cannons and torpedo launchers struck out ferociously at the barely detectable radiation signature left behind by the dreadnought's proton fire. The shots struck the stealth ship, most being deflected by the rayproof coating but a few finding purchase and melting into the dense armor beneath it.

"Yes!" Tarsik shouted, knowing that those heat signatures would only make the dreadnought even more visible to scanners.

"The *Gronshu* is moving." Emily reported, but it wasn't necessary. They could both see her rockets flare to maximum output. One of them sputtered momentarily, causing both of the spectators aboard the *Feather* to hold their breath. A few seconds later it flashed back to life and appeared to remain operational this time.

"See you after this is all over 'other me'", Eyepatch's voice boomed over the radio, "but as promised...here's our parting gift."

With no visible warning blueish/white beams erupted in pairs from several emitter banks too small to discern on the side of the *Gronshu's* hull.

Tarsik and Faust cheered as they witnessed the lepton beams not only strike the enemy dreadnought but also apparently slice through her armor with ease. Several small explosions rippled across the stealth ship's hull and her cannons ceased their hail of fire. Then there was a singular large flash of light as one of Kurian's atomics made contact.

Ten megatons inside an atmosphere is an incredible amount of energy that can flatten an entire city, in space however the vast majority of the explosive force expands outward and away from the target harmlessly. Still, even a small percentile of ten megatons does a whole lot of damage. The Interplanetary Holdings black project *Calypso* was, in an instant, venting atmosphere from five decks and was so thoroughly saturated with gamma radiation that her stealth technology was rendered completely useless.

"Ferricus you blithering buffoon I'll have your head on a pike!" Tali screeched as she marched forcefully onto the bridge of the *Calypso* as it limped away from the field of battle.

Hadant strode up to her with the full intention of laying the arrogant little bitch onto the deck with a backhanded slap but he noticed the armed guards a few steps behind her and restrained himself, but only just. He had spent the better part of a decade helping design the *Calypso* and overseeing her construction, not to mention the three years or so prior to that he'd wasted shopping around trying to find someone with the stones, and even more importantly the capital, to build such a warship.

The design and construction of the *Calypso* was supposed to be his legacy, his mark on the future of galactic politics, but the unholy alliance he'd been forced to accept with the Frazian girl had blown up in his face. He found himself so enraged with her that his head and body spines rose up on their own accord, a function of his Glintarin autonomic nervous system. The two guards apparently knew what the reaction meant, as they promptly raised their proton rifles to bear on him.

"You were ordered to destroy all of them flat out but you chose to defy me so that you could test out your little toy."

"You'll have to forgive me if I value my life's work and dozens of innocent lives over your childish games little girl!"

She gritted her teeth and with a scream of frustration slapped the aging Glintarin squarely across the cheek. She'd been careless though and one of his uplifted chin-spines neatly sliced her hand as it recoiled. She grasped it and watched as yellow-tinged blood welled up from the cut and drops of it began to spatter the deck.

"Oh look everyone," Hadant spat through gritted fangs, his golden eyes afire with sarcasm, "the girl who would be a god still bleeds after all!"

"Kill him!" Tali screamed to her attendants, her voice nearly breaking with a mixture of frustration and embarrassment.

The sound of proton rifles being primed to fire caused several of the captains' people to jump into action. They were loyal to him and that was by design. Hadant had been clever enough to have hand-picked his bridge crew. All of them had backgrounds in either law enforcement or organized militia. Simons, the large dark-complected human who served as command liaison to the engineering crew, jumped up and grabbed one of the guards from behind. He lifted the man off of the deck and tossed him at his compatriot. Their rayproof armor suits clattered against one another and they collapsed into a heap with an almost comical cacophony of sounds. Sera Nadal, the operations officer dove across the floor for one of the rifles and Simons snatched up the other. The two guards were at gunpoint before they could recover enough to reach their sidearms.

Hadant eyed Tali Asaddan'fal'fa'falool up and down. Her arrogant bravado had evaporated in an instant and he saw that what stood before him was little more than a petulant child. Still overwhelmed with anger he cocked his hand back and slapped her with all of his might, knocking her to the deck at his feet.

"Aaahhh!" she roared, clutching the cheek where the old captain had just struck her. "My father will have you put out of an airlock you prickly old hedgehog!"

"Get her up!" he barked at Simons.

The liaison officer slung the rifle and did as he was told. She protested as he grappled with her, but her efforts were futile.

Hadant strode up to her, his ferocity replaced with a playful snideness.

"So Tali, you want to be a goddess do you?" he grabbed her jaw in his hand and shook it a bit as he spoke, "That planet right there..." he pointed to one of the auxiliary screens which was displaying an image of Dathon VII, "...it's yours now isn't it? You're the goddess of the reformation aren't you?"

She said nothing and only glared at him in contempt.

"You want your planet so bad then I say you can have it." the captain looked up at Simons, "Toss her in a shuttle and cast her adrift."

The man's eyes went wide, "Sir...should we?!" Simons gasped. "She's the daughter of..."

"My order was clear." Hadant said, turning his back to the girl. He paused for a moment, turned to face her again, then violently snatched the small pouch off of her belt."

"Ferricus!" she screamed, her eyes pleading with him. "Please, don't do this."

The old Glintarin's lip curled up in anger but he took a deep breath and let it fade away. He gave a dismissive wave of his hand and with that Simons dragged her off of the bridge kicking and screaming the entire way. As the spectacle subsided Ferricus Hadant made his way back to the captain's chair and sat in it heavily. He looked around the bridge at his people carrying on the task of coordinating repair efforts.

"Let's see what the Dathonians think of their new goddess when she arrives alone and suffering from withdrawal." he muttered to himself.

34\\

The *Feather's* landing skiffs touched down onto the deck of the genesis engine's landing bay, their clanging sounds audible only inside the cockpit of the *Feather* itself as the force shield that maintained atmosphere inside the bay was clearly turned off and the entire space was open to vacuum.

Behind her the pilot could hear Captain Tarsik readying the gear they would take with them. She heard the familiar whine of his spiral ray pistol's power cell as he cycled it, checking the charge. Then there was the sound of a regular proton pistol having a fresh energy mag inserted.

"Bubble." Tarsik said as he handed her a helmet. She took it from him and, after quickly pinning her hair in place, slid it over her head. The Service uniform she'd changed into before leaving the *Gronshu* responded to the presence of the helmet like it was designed to. What looked like little more than a cloth uniform was actually a highly advanced piece of kit that was capable of maintaining atmosphere, deflecting glancing blows from knives, spears, and other edged weapons, and could even absorb moderate amounts of radiation, electrical discharge, and other forms of energy in order to keep the wearer safe.

The collar of the uniform reached up, as if by magic, and made contact with the polymer bubble she wore on her head. Slipping her gloves on the sleeves responded similarly by attaching themselves to the gloves before the entire outfit performed a quick self-check to ensure that all seals were stable.

"Sidearm." Tarsik announced as he handed her a weapon.

She did not hear him at first as her helmet filled with the familiar sound of the chime which told her that all seals had passed the diagnostic. Noticing him holding the weapon outstretched she nodded, took it from him, and then slapped it into place on her right hip where the automatic magnetic holster would hold it secure until it sensed the presence of a gloved hand trying to remove it for use. She touched a button on her belt and watched as the lights on her boots cycled; orange for power check, green for ready, then red for active as she felt her feet pulled down to the floor.

Looking over she saw that the captain had also managed to get his helmet on and was fiddling with the tele-wave on his belt.

"Can you hear me Faust?"

She nodded, still checking her gear. "Aye sir. Loud and clear."

At this point, only minutes away from confronting Essa Von Braun, the two spacers were all business. It seemed to both though neither would admit it, that during their brief conversations aboard the *Gronshu* and those tense moments aboard the *Feather* that the ember of a dialogue between them had begun to glow. Both knew what they had to do, knew that the time for talking had passed, and though some doubts about the future of their working relationship lingered both had an innate trust in the others' abilities. Neither worried about the next few minutes, knowing that they would face whatever came with a colleague that had their back.

Von Braun's most recent transmission fresh in their minds the two did not even bother with the cockpit ladder, deciding instead to simply slide down the fuselage and land directly on the deck.

"This is Essa Von Braun to the *Calypso*. Tell that fussy brat Tali that I'm about to turn her promised paradise into a lifeless smoldering hunk of rock and there's nothing she can do about it."

The message had been brief and to the point. Von Braun planned on overloading the genesis engine and torching the biosphere of the planet below. There were over a million Dathonians down there. Tarsik and Faust could not allow that to happen.

The metal plates of their boots would have resounded loudly in the landing bay had there been any air for the sounds to travel through. Tarsik looked over at Emily, "You ready for this Faust?"

"You're damned right I am." she sneered, "Let's go get this bitch."

Tarsik wasted only a fraction of a second on a smile and then patted her on the shoulder before breaking into a full run for the door with the pilot in close step behind him. They could see that the door's panel, like everything in the landing bay, had been powered down from somewhere else on the genesis engine, there would be no finesse involved with getting it open. Mid-sprint both spacers reached for their sidearms, brought them to bear on the door, and opened fire. The first blast from Tarsik's spiral ray pistol vaporized several millimeters of titanium into a cloud of fine metallic mist which three shots from Faust's proton pistol illuminated as the proton bursts struck the door as well. Still running full steam Tarsik used his thumb to switch the spiral ray up to its highest level and squeezed off a shot. This blast struck at the same time as Faust's second barrage and seemed to do the trick. The door in front of them vaporized completely and, had it not been for their magnetic boots, the quick outpouring of air would have sent them tumbling backwards out of the landing bay to float off into the vastness of space.

The escaping atmosphere came at them in such a torrent that it caused Faust to lose her grip on her weapon and nearly caused Tarsik to lose his grip on the spiral ray. Recovering quickly they knew that another inner door would soon be closing to seal off the breach so they once again broke into full sprint. Bolting through the remnants of what used to be the bay door they surveyed the scene quickly. To their left seemed to be a long hallway that went on for some ways until darkness rendered the rest of it invisible but to their right, only about ten meters distant, was a rapidly closing inner door. They immediately made for it but it was already more than halfway down from ceiling and would meet the floor in a matter of seconds.

Seeing Faust pull ahead of him in the rush Tarsik knew that he would never make it in time and it was quickly looking like Faust might not make it through either.

"Emily I'm going to do something stupid, just trust me and get under that door!"

"Aye." she shouted out between heavy breaths. Though she had no idea what the captain was about to do she knew him to have good instincts and she trusted that they would be right."

Running as fast as his considerable mass would allow him to Tarsik reached for the portable force-shield generator that he'd *borrowed* from Aeolus Station, unhooked it from his belt, flipped it on, and then slung it down the corridor as if he were playing an old Earth game of bowling.

Faust saw the device with its shimmering energy field slide past her and finally knew what she was supposed to do. It slid under the door in front of her and there was a considerable flash of light as the powerful door smashed down onto the device's force-shield. Without the slightest hesitation Faust dropped into a dive and slid through the opening that the captain's gadget was temporarily keeping open.

Recovering she spun and saw Tarsik's heavy boots approaching the door. The portable force-shield generator was doing its best to resist the power of the door servos but it appeared to be losing the battle.

Captain Tarsik dropped to the deck and looked through the opening at Faust. He had to keep shielding his eyes, as the force-shield continued to flash as it slowly lost ground to the powerful door mechanism.

"It's too small Faust, I can't fit!" he cried out over the tele-wave, "I'm going to let it seal and find another way around."

Faust nodded.

With that Tarsik reached for the MU-9 stunner on his belt, pulled it free, and then slid it under the door.

"You've got this Emily!" were his final words before he reached for the portable force-shield generator and deactivated it, allowing the door to close. Faust laid there in silence for a moment, the air around her still now, no longer rushing out toward the emptiness of space. The corridor was dark, lit only by what seemed to be emergency safety lighting.

"No time!" the words in her head snapped her back into action. She snatched up the stunner and placed it into the magnetic holster where her proton pistol had resided only moments before then jumped to her feet and shot off down the corridor, removing and tossing her helmet aside as she ran.

Tarsik pulled himself to his feet and lifted his gloved left hand to wipe at the film of fine dust particulates that had been ejected from the interior of the genesis engine and now coated the exterior of his helmet. He was thankful that nothing larger had come barreling out of the depths of the giant machine, like a tool that had been forgotten inside during construction. With the velocity of the escaping atmosphere it could have shattered his helmet and left him gasping for breath in the cold vacuum of space.

Reaching down he felt for one of the area lamps that he'd attached to his belt before disembarking the *Feather*. He pulled one of the devices free and tossed it at the wall where it affixed itself with an electromagnetic field. A moment later it flickered to life and illuminated the corridor. He looked down at the portable force-shield generator that was still grasped tightly in his right hand. Physically the device appeared no worse for wear but he knew that it was the internal field coils that were likely to have absorbed any damage rather than the shiny metallic casing.

"Come on baby." he said in a low tone, pressing the activation switch. It hesitated for a fraction of a section before popping to life. "Good." he said, again to no one but himself.

He placed it back onto his belt and then felt to make sure that his pistol was still in its holster. It was.

"Now, how in space-blasted hell do we get in there without decompressing the space behind Faust?"

He looked around the corridor. There were no ventilation ducts that he could make out and nothing that looked like access panels to crawl spaces. That left only one direction to head, back past the busted landing bay door and into the corridor that stretched on for a long ways behind him. Happy that his suit and his gear were still functional he plucked the area light from the bulkhead and placed it onto the small metallic pad on the top of his left-hand glove where it magnetized and stuck in place, automatically switching over to beam mode as it had been designed to do when worn on the body.

The captain shined the light down the corridor but its beam could not penetrate any further than the dim emergency lighting of the corridor itself already allowed him to see.

"Gonna have to hoof it." he thought to himself and with that set off in a trot.

"Well, that was easy." Emily Faust muttered to herself as the indicator light for the lift she'd summoned illuminated. Her hopes were dashed only moments later, however, when the door to the lift began to open only to immediately and forcefully close again.

"No no no, it's just me. I'm friendly. You can trust me." she said aloud in a placating tone as if the lift would hear her and respond in turn.

She pressed the button again but this time instead of lighting up green as it had before it lit up red and an angry warbling sound came from the speaker next to it.

"And now Essa knows I'm here...great."

As Tarsik approached the area where the emergency lighting began to fall off, what felt like at least 50 meters or so from the landing bay door, he began to be able to discern what looked like another door in the darkness. Shining his lamp on it confirmed this, but the door was marked with the word "DANGER" written in Standard as well as several other scripts, some he recognized, some he did not.

"Hmmph." he groaned as he strode up to it, "that probably means you're an airlock to some section that is still under construction and open to space...in which case I'm fine, or I'm about to come face to face with an unshielded reactor or some other thing that's going to pretty much kill me on the spot."

His gloved finger prodded the door's button which prompted a small screen next to it light up with another message of warning, "Exposed vacuum beyond this airlock. Confirm."

"Well, that answers that." he thought, then pressed the button to acknowledge the message.

The door slid up into the ceiling and presented him with a fairly standard looking airlock which illuminated with dull blue lighting as he entered. The door closed behind him and as he went through the confirmation with the second door he half expected it to open to the exterior of the massive genesis engine but was pleasantly surprised when he was presented instead with what looked to be an unfinished interior section.

He was surrounded by what appeared to be massive amount of scaffolding that stretched off into the distance and the flicker of a vibrant green light source from above drew his gaze upwards. The scaffolding rose what looked like no less than three or four hundred meters above his head and somewhere up there, near the very top, he could make out what looked to be a gantry of sorts that held the source of the eerie green glow. It looked to be the core of a massive magnetically contained reactor. That was the heart of the genesis engine and that was where Essa would be.

Tarsik checked to make sure that there was indeed atmosphere around him before removing his helmet and laying it on the deck. It was going to be one hell of a climb and he was already very much starting to regret having brushed off the doctor every time he'd instructed his captain to incorporate more cardio into his workouts.

Faust had stolen a glance at her chronometer when she'd first begun her efforts to hack into the control systems of the lift and was furious with herself that nearly ten whole minutes had elapsed by then time she'd gotten the space-blasted thing to cooperate. Now she tensed herself as the lift's indicator showed that it was approaching the control deck. She heard the material of her gloves creek as she lifted the MU-9 stun pistol to the ready position and tightened her grip on it. There was a quick "boong" as the lift came to a stop and, faster than she'd expected, the doors slid open with a pneumatic hiss.

Laid out in front of her was a massive open chasm, a giant upside-down teardrop shaped chamber of which she was nearly at the top of. A narrow catwalk of metal grating with sturdy looking handrails stretched out from the lift to the center of the space where it met two other catwalks that came from points each one-hundred and twenty degrees apart from one another. In the center was a circular catwalk that appeared to surround what she could only describe as an open-air fusion reactor with a pulsating green orb of incredible brightness at its center. She could see Essa at one of the control consoles that ringed the circular part of the catwalk. Her back was to Faust.

The pilot could see that there was a shield of tinted transparent titanium above the control consoles that prevented operators from being blinded by the brilliance of the reactor core and Essa seemed to be looking through it, not down at the console in front of her.

"Did she not detect me hacking the lift?" Faust thought to herself.

Slowly the pilot stepped forward. There was quite some distance between her and Von Braun and the deep thrumming of the core echoing inside the chasm should mask any small sounds she might make, but with only a less-than-lethal weapon at her disposal Faust was taking no chances.

She continued on, placing one foot in front of the other, her weapon bearing on the madwoman's back the entire way. Then, at about five meters from her target she saw Von Braun suddenly look down at the console. She realized that Essa might have seen her reflection in the tinted shield, and dropped into a roll just in time to dodge a proton blast from an as-yet unseen defense turret that was positioned over the lift that she'd just come from.

In an instant Von Braun spun on her heels and drew her weapon. Faust knew what kind of sidearm Essa carried and had no intention of getting hit by it but she had little choice other than to turn and fire on the defense turret, for it would not miss her again.

The blueish white blast from the stunner dissipated into the robotic turret and the pilot worried that it might not carry enough charge to disable the device but as she spun back around to face the disgraced Service captain she caught sight of it in her peripheral vision shooting forth a barrage of sparks. The stunner had indeed overloaded the mechanism, at least temporarily. Faust's sense of victory was short-lived, however, as before she could bring her sidearm to bear on Von Braun the woman squeezed off a shot of her own. The bolt from the dreaded KA7Z splashed across Emily's chest at an oblique angle, enough of a glancing blow that the shot did not penetrate her Service uniform. Faust sincerely hoped that it had also deflected enough of the shot's energy to prevent her from dying a slow death by radiation poisoning.

Answering back Faust fired off three rounds from the stunner, all of which Essa managed to evade, but it was enough to put her on the defense. She was ducking behind control consoles and only blindly firing back in an effort to get herself to better cover.

"Come out Essa, this is over!" Faust shouted over the thrum of the reactor.

"It'll be over when one of us is lying dead on the deck my dear." was the response.

The pilot could no longer see Von Braun. She'd made it behind a bank of consoles that were tall enough to allow her to move around undetected so long as she remained crouched. Emily's blue eyes darted from left to right, anticipating the attack that she knew would come. Von Braun was wily for sure, and even more savage, but at no less than twice Faust's age her reflexes weren't what they once were. The pilot hoped that would give her the edge she needed.

Essa's blonde head popped up a little further over to the right than Emily had expected but she reacted instinctively and deftly dodged a shot that had been aimed straight at her heart. Whirling around she brought the MU-9 to bear on her target and squeezed off a single shot. Von Braun had anticipated the return fire and moved to evade but she wasn't fast enough. The stun blast caught her in the upper portion of her right arm. The KA7Z fell from her grasp and clattered to the grating below as the entire limb went numb. Not wasting a moment Faust rushed forward and made sure that Essa knew she was dead to rights. With the stunner pointed right at Von Braun's sternum the pilot cried out, "Get up! Kick the pistol over to me!"

With no recourse Von Braun did as she was instructed. She rose slowly, clutching her right arm, and then looked down at her sidearm laying on the catwalk before her. A part of her wanted desperately to dive for it but she knew that with only her left arm functioning properly her chances of performing the maneuver and hitting her target with the first shot had just dramatically decreased to the point of irrelevance. Besides, she had another trick up her sleeve, quite literally. With a scowl she kicked the KA7Z toward the young pilot's feet.

Faust glanced over at the readout on the nearest console. There was a timer running and it was counting down with forty-eight seconds remaining.

"The overload," she shouted over the ambient noise, "shut it down now!"

Essa scoffed, "Or what sweetie? You'll stun me?"

Von Braun slowly began to inch her left hand toward the plasma derringer strapped into the secret holster on her back.

"How about I stun you and then toss your limp corpse

over the side of this railing?" Faust smirked, "I'll make sure you're awake for the whole thing but too stunned to move a muscle."

"Ooh," Von Braun cooed, "saucy! I like you girl." she smiled.

Faust saw through the facade, noticed the moment in Essa's eyes when she made the decision to kill. She lifted the stunner's sights to point directly at Von Braun's trachea but before she could pull the trigger a large form came down hard on the catwalk in front of her.

"Captain!" her inner monologue cried out, but then aloud, "Watch out, she's got a...!"

Tarsik was already ahead of her, he lifted his force-shield and snapped it on a split-second before Essa managed to free the derringer and fire off a shot. The plasma bolt ricocheted off of the force-shield out into the cavernous room. Desperate, Von Braun followed it up the weapon's second and final shot. This one the shield deflected right back at her and the discharge struck her in the collarbone.

"Aaahhhh!" Essa screamed and released the derringer down from her grip. It tumbled into the abyss below. She clutched at the fresh wound and howled, "Tarsik you son of a bitch!".

Her face flushed with anger and she rushed forward full force without thinking. Tarsik grinned, his shield still out in front of him...at least until it flickered and went dead. Surprised he tossed it aside and braced himself for the impact. Essa slammed into Captain Tarsik with enough force that she knocked him over the railing and they both went tumbling into the chasm below.

Faust scrambled to her feet, certain that both were as good as dead, but she sighed in relief as she spotted them only about ten meters below on one of the auxiliary catwalks that ran across the width of the vast interior space. They were likely pretty badly injured, but they'd survive...she hoped, at least for the captain's sake.

Remembering the countdown she sprang into action and ran over to the console she'd spotted only moments before.

"Override! Override!" she shouted at herself internally. "Where is the fraggin override?!"

"Faust!" she heard the captain call down from below. She brushed it aside, focusing instead on the current situation.

Her eyes darted across the panel. There, in large yellow letters, was a switch labeled "emergency shutdown." She flipped the switch with such bravado she feared she might snap its shaft but nothing happened. "Captain!" she called out, "We have a problem up here, the emergency shutdown isn't working!"

Von Braun was injured, considerably moreso than himself, Tarsik thought. There was fresh bright red blood on her lips. He was pretty sure that she'd struck the safety rail of the catwalk they now found themselves on with her chest during the fall, likely causing massive internal hemorrhaging.

He squeezed her hand, "How do we stop it? How do we stop it Essa?!"

She smiled then spat blood out in a spray, "You can't Captain, you can't. The reactor is past critical, the energy has to go somewhere."

"Faust!" Tarsik looked up at the catwalk above him and yelled out, "We can't stop it, energy has to go somewhere. I'm guessing that means either the planet burns or we do!"

Emily's mind raced, she knew that she'd sacrifice her own life for the million or so below in a heartbeat suddenly she latched onto a thought that she believed the captain had not. He said "the energy has to go somewhere". That could mean the overload, or they could direct it to detonate the genesis engine...but she realized that there was a third option. What was this station, what was it constructed to do?! It's a terraforming station! Let it do what it's supposed to do!

"Third option Captain!" she yelled out over the intensifying thrum of the reactor.

"Third option?!" Tarsik pleaded. The look in Von Braun's eyes told him instantly what Faust meant.

"No!!!" Essa cried out.

"Do I have the right to make this decision for literally a million people down there?" Emily Faust thought to herself. She glanced at the counter, only ten seconds left to decide. She steadied herself and spoke softly, "I see it now, command is about making the hard choices. They may be wrong but damnit somebody's got to make them!"

She flipped the switches that would redirect the terraforming beam back into proper alignment and with less than two seconds to spare smashed the button labeled *initiate*.

Tarsik had thought Essa unconscious laying next to him but suddenly she grasped the IPH insignia on her cowl and tore it free. With all of her remaining might she plunged the sharp end into Tarsik's left eye.

"AAAAHHHH!!!" the captain screamed in agony as he recoiled from the attack. The pulsating thrum of the reactor was growing to a deafening tidal roar. Von Braun was clinging onto the catwalk, her lower half dangling down over the edge. Tarsik's face snarled in rage and he cocked his boot back before slamming it into the woman's face.

"You...." he yelled, "fraggin...." he kicked her again, even harder, "bitch!!!" and with that his final blow caused her to lose her grasp on the grating and she went tumbling into the darkness below only to be swallowed up a fraction of a second later by the terraforming beam, a sight which, unshielded, was so intense it nearly cost the captain the vision in his other eye as well.

EPILOGUE

Sitting alongside the dry dock at the Lorandis orbital yards Tarsik and Faust let their legs dangle over the edge as they watched the activity swirling about the *Honshu*. The old girl was on her side, suspended by a massive overhead crane that would allow work to be done on the fins.

They'd been there for at least a half hour. Most of that time had been spent on idle chitchat or laughing at Ansul running around trying to keep up with all of the work being done. Occasionally he would shout at a random technician or pull the foreman aside to go over the design specs yet again.

Interplanetary Holdings was in hot water over the revelation that they'd financed and overseen construction of a prototype stealth warship. Their misfortune turned out to be a blessing for Captain Tarsik however, as they were doing everything they could to polish their reputation in the wake of the news. Not only had they kept their promise to repair the *Honshu* but they'd gone a step further and hired a prestigious design firm on Tersis to oversee the entire project.

"It's gonna take a while to get used to the new look." Faust remarked, referring to the proposed exterior changes the ship would be receiving.

"She'll still be the *Honshu*." Tarsik assured her.

Emily laughed, "Oh you thought I was talking about the ship?" she gestured to the captain's uncharacteristically casual attire, "I meant I don't know if I can get used to…this."

"Ha ha." Tarsik said dryly, then switched to a more serious tone. "I want you to know I'm proud of you Pilot. You did it. You made the tough call and you know what the means don't you?"

She smiled and brushed a loose bit of hair behind her ear before replying sarcastically, "That you assume I'm ready to come back to the *Honshu*?"

"You *are* coming back, aren't you?" he asked more coyly than she'd ever seen him speak.

The pilot allowed a small chuckle to escape. "You do realize that *Honshu* is going to be grounded for what, two months?"

"Hah, try three months…at least!"

"Really, that long?"

He nodded.

After a moment she decided that she'd avoided the question long enough. "You do realize that I have my own ship now, right?"

"The *Feather*?" he replied, "Yeah, and she's a fine little ship…"

"But she's no *Honshu* is what you were going to say right?"

He smiled and shrugged playfully.

"Say I do come back, will you ever trust me with her again?"

At that Tarsik had a visible reaction. He shifted his position so as to face her more directly.

"Emily you do know that from the moment you stepped on board I started grooming you to take over for me after I retire, don't you?"

She had indeed suspected as much but the typically

stoic Captain Tarsik had never come out and said it.

"You want me to take over Big Blue?" she asked with a grin.

"I can't think of anyone else for the job. Of course that's many *many* years from now. I've got a lot of fight left in me."

"I don't doubt it." she beamed. "Thank you sir."

"Oh look, here he comes again." Tarsik pointed to Ansul who was walking briskly alongside the dock foreman and apparently in the middle of a heated discussion.

"Yes, I know the difference between gilded and non-gilded biphasic transfer line but the question is do your people?"

Suddenly he noticed the Captain and Faust sitting alongside the dock and waved the man away. "We'll talk about it afterwhile."

"Yeah yeah." the man grumbled.

Ansul shook his head, "No 'yeah yeah', I'm serious. At least a couple of these guys I wouldn't trust to work on a go-cart."

"Ansul," the captain called out, "come and sit your ass down and leave these poor people alone."

"Did you two hear?!" the Martian asked as he walked up.

"Hear what?" Faust asked, somewhat taken aback by the worry she saw on Ansul's face. "That the chairman of IPH is being called to testify before the FW Grand Council because the commander of their stealth ship has gone rogue and half the galaxy is out hunting for it? Yeah."

The mechanic walked over to where they were sitting and kneeled next to his friends. "No, it's not that." he said, shaking his head somberly. He spoke softly as if to make sure no one else overheard. "Look, when the *Gronshu* left everything went back to normal, right?"

Tarsik didn't like where this was going. After the events at Dathon VII they'd been left with two major problems. First there was the issue of the dimensional bleed, and secondly the *Gronshu* apparently being stranded in their universe. They'd swung for the fences by proposing the wild idea that if the *Gronshu* flew into the Crux and engaged NC near the point that the two timelines were colliding that maybe they could not only return home but fix the dimensional rift at the same time. It had *seemed* to work.

"Yeah, well things are anything but normal." Ansul reached into his pocket and pulled out a folded piece of paper. "This," he said as he unfolded it, "is what I got when I tried to use some credit to buy a coffee this morning."

He handed the paper to Tarsik. The captain's eyes skimmed over it quickly and Faust became concerned when she saw his brow furrow in confusion. "What, does it say you're deceased or something?" she joked, trying to lighten the mood.

"No." Tarsik said, still staring at the printout, "It says that he's not a member of the Service, that he's a professor of astrophysics at the University of Mars."

Faust laughed. Surely it was a joke. She tore the paper from Tarsik's hands and read it herself.

"How is that possible?!" she asked, staring Ansul right in the eye.

"Best guess? We fixed the problem of the other dimension bleeding into this one but our actions in the past changed a few things. And that's not all."

He reached into a different pocket on his jacket and produced a second folded piece of paper.

"This one's much more disturbing." he warned.

Tarsik took it from him. Faust leaned in close to see what it said. It appeared to be a printout from a news article. The tagline read "WAR IN THE SMALL CLOUD!"

ABOUT THE AUTHOR

Michael Moreau is creator of series such as The Futureman Adventures, Rocket Riders of the 27th Century, and The Robert Carson Files. He is a life-long fan of science fiction and always dreamed of writing books of his own. He is a supporter of pulp-style fiction and a staunch advocate for self-publication. He is also a prolific filmmaker, photographer & artist.

More information can be found at:

www.mmoreau.net

THE YESTERDAY DILEMMA

OTHER WORKS BY THE AUTHOR

-The Futureman Adventures-
It Came From Tomorrow (2012)
Future Tales and Other Such Rubbish (2015)

-Rocket Riders of the 27th Century-
No Time Like the Future (2014)
Where the Stars Fall (2014)

-The Robert Carson Files-
A Case Most Peculiar (2015)

-Other-
Call Me Ogi (2015)
Sherlock Holmes: Monster Hunter (2016)

Made in the USA
Monee, IL
28 December 2023